WILD RODEO NIGHTS

Wilder Series 2

Sandy Sullivan

EROTIC ROMANCE

Siren Publishing, Inc.
www.SirenPublishing.com

A SIREN PUBLISHING BOOK
IMPRINT: Erotic Romance

WILD RODEO NIGHTS
Copyright © 2010 by Sandy Sullivan

ISBN-10: 1-60601-699-7
ISBN-13: 978-1-60601-699-2

First Printing: May 2010

Cover design by Jinger Heaston
All cover art and logo copyright © 2010 by Siren Publishing, Inc.

Printed in the U.S.A.

PUBLISHER
Siren Publishing, Inc.
www.SirenPublishing.com

DEDICATION

This is dedicated to the fans of *Wild Wyoming Nights*. Got to love those Wilder boys, so enjoy Cole's story.

WILD RODEO NIGHTS

Wilder Series 2

SANDY SULLIVAN
Copyright © 2010

Chapter One

"You son of a bitch!" The words were hissed so low next to his ear, Cole Wilder almost miss it against the thrum of the music.

Beer half way to his lips, he turned around slowly to meet the hazel eyes of the most beautiful woman he'd ever seen. Her brown hair hung to the middle of her back, curling slightly at the ends where it brushed at her shoulders. Cole propped his elbow on the bar and cocked his head to the side. "Pardon?"

"Bastard," she growled. "She's not even eighteen!"

Cole's eyes widened, and his thoughts raced backward to the last several weeks. He and Jimmy only arrived in this small town the night before, ready to ride at the rodeo this weekend. He didn't have a clue what this hellcat was talking about. Silver Ridge, South Dakota wasn't a regular stop for him.

"Ma'am, I really have no…"

"Don't you ma'am me." Her eyes sparkled like diamonds even in the muted light of the smoky bar when they raked him from head to toe, branding him with her stare. "She's knocked up, and you're responsible."

"Whoa! Wait just a damned minute here." All six feet towered over her smaller frame now, but that didn't stop her as she pressed one finger into the middle of his chest.

"Couldn't keep your dick in your pants long enough to find out how old she was?"

He backed up, putting a little distance between them, but she stepped closer, her heaving chest almost touching his. "Exactly who are you and who in hell are you talking about?"

A protective snarl left her lips and she growled, "Didn't even catch her name while you fucked her brains out?"

"I'll have you know, I've never went to bed with a woman whose name I didn't know first."

The sneer tugging at her mouth had him cocking his eyebrow when she obviously ignored his statement. "What she ever saw in you, I have no idea. If your dick is as short as your memory, it's a wonder you figured out how it worked and got her pregnant."

"Listen, lady. I haven't gotten anyone pregnant." He stepped back, but she continued to follow, until he bumped into the man behind him. "Are you always this sweet or is that tongue of yours normally as sharp as cheap tequila?"

"Only when it comes to defending my little sister and making sure the man who got her knocked up owns up to his responsibility."

"And her name?" Cole knew there was no way in hell he had gotten anyone pregnant. He was way too careful when he bedded a woman, but this little firebrand had him curious. She was fighting mad, hissing and scratching like a lioness defending her cub and from the moment she'd stuck her claws in him, he had been fascinated.

"Jessica Marsh ring any bells in that empty space between your ears?"

A sharp inhalation of breath echoed in the air behind him, and when Cole turned around to look at his friend, the white sheen of Jimmy's skin told him all he needed to know.

"Jim. Care to explain?"

"I—uh…"

"You?" Her eyes swung from him to Jimmy, who sat next to him and then back to meet his gaze. "You aren't Jimmy?"

"Sorry to disappoint you, but no."

She stepped back, embarrassment flushing her cheeks while her mouth worked and her jaw clamped so tight he was sure it probably ached.

"Oh, my God. I'm sorry. I thought…shit." She spun on her heels and disappeared through the crowd. The last sight he had of her, she turned around and shot him a heated glance across the room. When she disappeared into the night, he wasn't sure why, but he felt like his life had just taken an unexplainable turn he wasn't prepared for.

* * * *

The sun peeked through the thin curtains on the bedroom window, spreading a ribbon of gold across Carrie's face when she rolled over and groaned. Reaching across the bedside table, she smacked the alarm clock as it blared a country song. Sighing, she flipped the covers back and grumbled before she slowly rolled out of the bed and then stumbled toward the bathroom.

Steaming water filled the room with a foggy mist , obliterating her reflection in the mirror over the sink.

"It's a good thing I can't see what I look like right now. I probably look like death warmed over after those beers."

Slipping out of her t-shirt and shorts, she stepped into the stream of water with a heavy sigh. The water sluiced over her, traveling down her chest in rivulets when she tipped her head back.

I never should have gotten drunk last night, but damn! After ripping the guy in the bar, then finding out he was the wrong man…I felt like crap! And I didn't even confront the real guy responsible. Damn!

Finding out yesterday about her baby sister's pregnancy was enough to send her anger soaring into the clouds. Jessie only turned seventeen eight months ago and with a baby on the way, no father and no parents, Carrie was all she had.

What the hell am I going to do now?

"Get a grip, Carrie. First things first, you need to get the store open for the day. You need the money from the rodeo this weekend to make the bills this month." The pep talk did the job by boosting her spirits some when she started scrubbing her hair and washing her body. After rinsing clean, she grabbed a thinning towel and quickly dried off.

She slipped on her standard hip hugging jeans, tank top, and boots. Pulling her hair back in a ponytail, she swiped a little makeup across her cheeks before she walked out the door, headed for the shop.

When she pulled into the parking lot, a black Ford truck caught her attention and her eyes narrowed. She didn't recognize the vehicle. The other truck sitting nearby was Ken Webber's. The big dually truck, painted bright red, always stood out wherever it sat. Ken had been chasing her for years, and he made sure she knew it as well as anyone else within earshot. Coming by the store on a regular basis, he sometimes bought supplies, but he mostly hung out hoping she would relent and go out with him.

Grabbing her purse and keys, she slid out of her old Chevy and slammed the door behind her. She headed for the ribbed steel door, locked against any unwanted visitors, when she heard a voice behind her.

"Hey, Carrie."

She waved but didn't turn around when she heard Ken's voice. She didn't need his annoying presence right at the moment. Her priority had to be getting the store open before the rodeo contestants starting showing up wanting feed or whatever.

Pulling up the sliding door, she unlocked the front and headed for the office to grab the cash bag. The bell above the entrance tinkled when someone pushed it open and walked in.

Probably Ken. The strange truck could be another customer though.

"I'll be right there." She pulled open the small safe, grabbing the cash bag before she walked out and headed for the counter. Her eyes narrowed as she picked out the tall frame of a man looking at the selection of boots along the wall. With his back to her, she couldn't tell if it was a local or someone from the rodeo. She shrugged after studying him for a moment, sliding the fives and ones into the cash drawer before pushing it shut.

Ken slipped his elbows onto the counter, leaning heavily on the glass under them. The case held a wide array of silver belt buckles, silver jewelry, and accoutrements any rodeo rider would be proud to own.

"Hey, babe."

"Something I can get for you, Ken?"

"Yeah—you."

She rolled her eyes. "Sorry. I'm not on the available for purchase list. Anything else?"

A soft chuckle reached her ears as she shot a glance over her shoulder at the man she saw earlier. She cocked her head to the side, studying his back. The normal cowboy attire adorned his tall frame, complete with western shirt, Wranglers that hugged his lean hips, the standard black Stetson, and boots that obviously belonged to a rider if she was any judge.

Nice ass on him, too, she thought until her attention was brought back to the man in front of her.

An exaggerated sigh left Ken's lips before he took her hand in his. "Come on, Carrie, just dinner."

"No, Ken. I don't have time with the store and keeping an eye on Jess these days."

"You can close up a little early. Hell, with your parents not around anymore, there isn't anyone to tell you what to do now."

"That's it! Get out of my store—now!"

"Easy, girl." He put up his hands in surrender. "What the hell did I say?"

"Get. Out!"

Mumbling under his breath, he whispered, "Damn women anyway."

Once he was gone, she placed her hands on the counter and dropped her gaze to the floor at her feet. Taking in great gulps of air, she tried to calm the pain in her heart. Her parents died just over a year before in a terrible car accident, leaving her and Jess alone.

"Uh—excuse me. I hate to bug you, but I need a chinstrap for my bridle."

Her head snapped up at the sound of the voice.

Shit! It can't be!

The startled look on her face must have been hilarious when a slow smile spread across his full lips, revealing the dimples she hadn't noticed the night before.

"Well, hello again."

Great! This is all I need today.

The intense blue eyes of the man she wrongly accused of impregnating her teenage sister stared back.

Shit! The whole town is probably having a good laugh this morning about the scene at the bar last night.

Squaring her shoulders she asked, "What can I get for you?"

He leaned against the counter and repeated with a smile. "A chinstrap?"

"Yeah. Sorry. This way." She walked around the counter toward the other side of the store. A wide array of tack hung from every corner and every crevice available. "As you can see, there are several styles and colors. I'm sure you should be able to find something that matches."

"Thanks."

"You're welcome." She walked back to the counter, leaving him to sort through the selection. The hair on her arms stood on end when she turned and caught his gaze across the aisle before she turned back around to sort through receipts. Not that they needed sorting, but it gave her something to think about besides the man.

Several more customers came in, and she was lost in the shuffle of helping them with their purchasing until thirty minutes later. When the store cleared, he stood next to the register.

"Sorry. I didn't mean to leave you over there by yourself."

"No problem."

"Did you find what you were looking for?"

He held up the strap for her to see as he leaned on the counter, the ring on his pinky finger flashing in the overhead light.

"Ah. Good. Would you like for me to ring it up for you?"

"That'd be fine." Reaching into his back pocket for his wallet, he lifted his gaze to her and asked, "Can I ask you a question?"

She shrugged, punching the amount into the register. "Sure."

"Why did you accuse me of getting your sister pregnant? I haven't been in Silver Ridge since last year, plus I've never seen you before, and believe me, babe, I'd remember."

* * * *

Studying her for a second, Cole asked with a smile, "I saw one side of your sunny personality last night at the bar, and it doesn't seem to be any better this morning. Are you always this grumpy?" He let his appreciative stare roam over her brown hair, hazel eyes, and her full lips just begging to be kissed. His gaze moved a little further down, taking in the breasts pressed against the front of her shirt, not too large, but just enough to fill a man's hands.

She closed her eyes a moment before her gaze met his. "About last night…"

"Yeah. Wanna explain?"

She looked around to make sure there wasn't anyone else in the store before she leaned slightly forward, giving him an enticing view as her tank top gaped open.

"I just found out yesterday my baby sister is pregnant. She gave me a description of the guy, and I mistakenly thought it was you." She straightened and squared her shoulders. "Obviously you and your friend have similar features. I guess I assumed it was the better looking of the two of you. From what she told me, she met your friend a few months ago. I'm not sure exactly how they hooked up, but they obviously slept together during their short interlude."

He cocked an eyebrow when her offhanded compliment met his ears.

"As for my disposition this morning, I got a little drunk last night when I got home and I haven't had enough caffeine yet today."

"I see."

She hit a button of the register, and the drawer popped open with a ding. "Your total is nine fifty."

He pulled out a ten dollar bill from his wallet and handed it to her. "So you run this place all by yourself?"

"For now—yes." Slipping the money into the register, she pulled out two quarters, pushed the drawer shut, and handed him the change.

The bell over the door rang, drawing their attention to the older gentleman sauntering in.

"Howdy, Ms. Carrie. How's things?"

"Good, Jeb. What can I get you today?"

"I need six bales of that Orchard Grass hay you have in the corner, two salt blocks, and a bag of rabbit food."

"Coming right up." Her gaze met Cole's again. "Sorry. I need to take care of this. He's one of my best customers."

"Of course. I need to go check my horse anyway." He held up the chinstrap and said, "Thanks for saving my ride."

"No problem. Good luck today." He stepped back when she moved from behind the counter.

"Thanks."

With one last lingering look over her shoulder, she disappeared into what he assumed to be a storage area and was gone.

Chapter Two

The customers finally slowed down a little when the rodeo events began, and she sighed. She hated when she had to work alone, but Jess wasn't feeling well these days and Carrie had no other help. Her other helper called in sick, too. She couldn't blame him. Rodney sounded terrible on the phone, but if she found out he was skipping work to be at the rodeo, she'd kick his tail.

The bell tinkled over the door. Standing down one aisle helping a young girl and her mother looking at some cowboy hats, she couldn't tell who came in. They sold all kinds of flashy things during the events, but hers were cheaper, bringing the participants and spectators alike to her store.

"I'm not sure if I like this one or the other one." The girl's nasally voice grated on her nerves as she whined.

"I think both look good on you, but this one fits your personality better." She turned to see who had come in, but she couldn't spot them over the shelves. "You keep looking, and I'll be back in a few minutes."

The girl's mother and Carrie exchange exasperated looks before she smiled and headed back for the front. Approaching the counter, she was startled to see the gorgeous cowboy from this morning standing by the register.

Mmm…I wonder what he's doing back here.

"Forget something?"

"Nope. I brought a peace offering." He held up the biggest cup of coffee she'd ever seen.

She chuckled. "I should be giving you a peace offering since I ripped into you."

"Well, I figured this way you'd get your mega dose of caffeine, and I could see you again."

Trepidation rippled down her back and she narrowed her eyes. *A come on?*

"Thanks for the coffee, but I'm not..."

"This isn't a come on, Carrie." Her name rolling off his tongue sent shivers down her spine and goose bumps across her arms.

"Well, I can't let you buy me coffee anyway. I don't even know your name." She pulled two dollars out of the register to hand to him, but he shoved it back at her.

"It's Cole. Cole Wilder."

"Just here for the rodeo, Cole?" She took the packets of sugar and cream he brought, doctoring up the strong brew.

"Yeah."

"What events?"

"Calf roping and bulls."

"Ah, An adrenaline junkie."

The bell tinkled again and she groaned.

"I'll get it," he offered, turning to approach the customers as her gaze followed his muscled back.

He didn't just offer to help my customers, did he?

She watched him use his devastating good looks to charm the woman who came in, taking her order, before he turned back toward her asking where the things were. Directing his movements, she told him where to get the things Mrs. Roberts asked for before he grabbed a large sack of feed and hefted it onto his shoulder.

"I didn't realize you had such a nice looking young man helping you these days, Carrie."

"Um...yeah." Tearing her eyes away, she jotted down the order. "Do you want me to put this on your account, Mrs. Roberts?"

"Sure, honey. That'd be fine." The older woman looked at Cole and asked, "Would you be a dear and take the sack out to the truck for me?"

"Of course, ma'am."

Her appreciative gaze followed his nicely exposed backside when he walked out the door, and she sighed.

More customers rolled in right behind the woman, never really giving her a chance to say anything more to him. He jumped right in, taking care of anyone he could as her startled gaze followed him around the store. Cole quickly learned where everything was while she manned the register and he filled orders. Before she knew it, it was time to close the store. Following the last customer to the door, she thanked them for their purchases and locked the door. She turned the sign and leaned heavily against the panel for a moment, closing her eyes before she released a heavy sigh.

"Is that it?"

Her eyes opened slowly. "Yeah—finally." Realization hit her square in the face. "Oh no! You were supposed to ride today, weren't you?"

"Yeah." His shoulders lifted in a shrug. "No big deal."

She smacked her forehead. "I can't believe I let you help me and miss your ride."

He took her hand in his and softly caressed the back with his fingers. "It's okay. There'll be others."

She nervously pulled her hand back, wiping her palm on her jeans. "I know all about how riders are. You're just trying be nice even after the dressing down I gave you last night."

"No, Carrie. I wanted to help." He smiled, showing off those gorgeous dimples when he put his hand on the door next to her shoulder.

She shifted uncomfortably before pushing away from the panel behind her and heading back toward the counter. "Well, I still shouldn't have let you, but thank you anyway. I wouldn't have been able to keep up today without your help."

"You are most certainly welcome. Besides, I'm not afraid of hard work."

"I kind of gathered that." She grabbed the money from the register, slipped it inside the bag, and headed toward the office. Pulling open the safe, she slid the bag back inside, shut the heavy door and spun the dial. Grabbing her purse and her keys, she looked up to see him standing in the doorway. She stopped in front of him, expecting him to step aside, but he didn't move for a moment. Her gaze ricocheted up to his with a questioning tilt of her head.

He finally stepped back and gave her enough room to pass but not by much. Her breath caught when her breasts almost touched his chest. The slow, steady, sexy-as-sin grin rippled across his lips for a moment before she cleared her throat and moved past him.

"You could probably still catch some of the rodeo. The events go on for several more hours."

"No. I'm not in the mood tonight."

What are you in the mood for? She shook her head to clear her thoughts. *The last thing I need is a temporary man in my life, but I should thank him for helping me.*

She headed for the steel door with him on her heels. Once it was locked and secure, he moved toward her truck with her. Turning to look at his handsome face, she was shocked at the heat in his gaze. When it traveled down her body, she shivered.

"If you aren't going to the rodeo, can I fix you dinner? It's the least I can do for your help today."

The slow smile was back, showing the dimples in his cheeks. Her thoughts quickly went haywire as she wondered what it would be like to lick those devastating indentations.

"Sure. I'd like that."

"Okay. You can follow me back to the house."

"No problem." He headed for his truck while she slid into hers and started the engine. Keeping him in her rear view mirror, she pulled out onto the highway. Within several minutes, they drove down the long driveway surrounded by obvious electric fencing, beautiful black horses grazed in the distance as the sun went down over the hill behind them. Parking in front of the porch, they both climbed out and headed for the door.

He walked up behind her when she reached the front of the house. "Nice place."

"Thanks." She frowned when her gaze found the still dark windows.

"What's wrong?"

"Nothing, I guess. I just expected Jess to be here, but there aren't any lights on."

Walking into the large living room, she set her purse on the table and yelled, "Jess?"

Silence met her ears, nothing to tell her the other young woman was home. She turned to look at the man standing in the room with her before she chewed her lip. *Great! Now I'm alone with him. I really hoped Jess would be here.* "Can I get you something to drink?"

"Sure, whatever you have is fine."

"Okay. I'll be right back."

She walked into the kitchen and pulled open the refrigerator. After she grabbed a couple of beers, she shut it and headed back into the living room.

He stood near the fireplace mantel looking through the several pictures sitting there. She took in his appearance before he realized she had come back in the room. Standing at six feet, his blond hair curled slightly while it brushed the back of his neck near his collar, and her fingers itch to comb through it.

I wonder if they are as soft as they appeared.

The muscles of his back and arms pulled at the material of his shirt, stretching it taut. Her gaze wandered down his back to his firm ass, encased in the standard Wranglers of a cowboy, down to the boots on his feet. When his hand touched hers earlier at the store, the calluses on his fingers brushed against her palm, sending tingles of awareness up her arm.

With a grumble, she pulled her gaze from his enticing form and stepped closer, holding out the beer in her hand. He turned, and his intense blue eyes captured hers, sending her heart into overdrive while the errant organ slammed against her ribs.

"Thanks."

"I'll see what's available for dinner."

She hurried back into the kitchen and stopped at the counter, taking a deep breath to still her racing heart. Lifting her head, she pulled open the refrigerator again and grabbed the two steaks she took out yesterday for dinner. "It'll have to do, I guess," she mumbled before she placed them on the counter to make a little marinade.

* * * *

He let his gaze linger on her backside as she walked back toward the kitchen. Lifting the long neck to his lips, he felt the cold liquid slide down his throat, settling somewhere in his empty stomach. She fascinated him, and he wasn't quite sure why. She was pretty. He'd give her that.

Hell, who am I kiddin'? She's gorgeous!

The ends of her brown hair brushed the middle of her back even tied back in a ponytail, and he wondered what it would feel like wrapped around him. Beer lingered on his lips, and he wiped it off with the back of his hand before he shifted his stance, trying to relieve the pressure against the fly of his jeans.

It had been a while since he'd been with a woman.

Too damned long, obviously.

He groaned silently, wondering what her breasts would taste like when he licked her nipples. Her back was toward him when he reached the doorway between the kitchen and the living room.

"Steak okay with you? I've got a gas grill in the back. We can throw them on there."

"Sounds good," he said from not far behind her. She jumped and put her hand on her chest before she turned around. "Sorry. I didn't mean to scare you. I got lonesome out there by myself."

"It's okay. I just didn't hear you come in. You're pretty quiet even wearing cowboy boots." A smile flittered across her lips, making her eyes dance in the florescent lighting over their heads.

He leaned against the door jamb and watched her putter around the kitchen, grabbing things from the refrigerator and the cabinets. "How long have you lived here?"

"All my life. My parents bought this place thirty years ago, so both my sister and I were born here. Not in the house itself, of course, but here in town."

"You've never been out of Silver Ridge?"

She shot him a strange look. "Of course I've been out of Silver Ridge. I'm not some backwoods country girl, you know."

"I didn't mean to offend you. I'm curious."

"I've only been out of South Dakota a few times, though. My dad used to take us into Wyoming sometimes to buy cattle or horses." She turned her attention back to the tomato while she sliced it. "So— where are you from? I mean, obviously you get around some since you ride."

"Wyoming originally. Now…wherever the rodeo takes me most of the time."

"Where in Wyoming?"

She placed the steaks on a plate and motioned for him to follow with a nod of her head.

He held the screen door for her as she passed next to him on the way to the patio.

"Outside Laramie." He took the seat she pointed to as she set the plate near the barbeque.

"Really. Interesting."

"Why?"

She shrugged. "My dad spent a lot of time in Laramie, actually." Once the steaks were on the grill and she pulled the lid down, she took the seat across from him. "Are you parents still there?"

"Yeah. Mom and Dad live in town now, but one of my brothers runs the ranch with his new wife." He dropped his gaze from hers for a moment when he thought about Chase and Abby, a smile rippling across his lips. Silver Ridge South Dakota was his first stop after their wedding several months ago. He spent the winter helping Chase and Abby as well as visiting his parents and his brother Justin, but riding season started.

"*One* of your brothers?"

"Yep. I'm the youngest boy. Chase is the middle child, and he just got married a few months ago. Justin is my older brother, and he lives in Nevada. Then there is Jamie. She's the baby of the family. She still lives with my parents in Laramie most of the time with her daughter."

A sad look crossed her eyes a moment before they met his again. "I wish I would have had more siblings. It's just me and Jess."

"What happened to your parents?"

She didn't answer at first, but he saw tears welling up in her eyes. He had the insane urge to pull her close and wipe away the sadness, but she squared her shoulders, stood up, and walked several feet away.

"They were killed in a car accident about a year ago." She rubbed her arms, her back to him. "I was at college when I got the call. I have to take care of Jess now until she's at least eighteen. Not like I'll turn my back on her after that, but she'll at least be out of high school then." She spun back around, and the anger in her eyes took him back for a moment. "Thanks to your friend, there is one more complication with her being pregnant. By the way, I would appreciate if you would help me pin him down and make him take responsibility for the child she now carries."

He stood and walked to her side, laid his hands on her shoulders and kneaded the soft muscles for a moment. "Carrie, I'm sorry. I can't imagine having to be responsible for another when it's forced on you like this has been, but don't hold it against me, okay? If I could make him do the right thing, I would, but I can't. He's a friend, but I can't make him do anything he doesn't want to."

She sighed and stepped back. "I'm sure you would, Cole. You seem like the kind of man who wouldn't walk away from his responsibilities, and I'm sorry. I just can't believe she was so careless and I don't mean to take it out on you."

Pulling open the grill, she flipped the steaks over. "I'll be right back. I need to get the potatoes in the microwave."

"Sure." Watching her move back into the house, protectiveness struck him hard, curling in his belly like nothing he had ever felt before. For some odd reason, he wanted to hold her and take away her cares and worries.

After a few minutes, she returned with another beer for him and one for herself. Taking the chairs again, she tucked her feet under her as the beer bottle dangled from her fingers. "So, I imagine you have a girl in every town."

He almost choked on his beer when his eyes met hers and he saw the twinkle in her gaze. "Not really, no." He laughed out loud.

"Yeah right! With those looks and those teasing dimples, I bet you have women falling all over you at every stop you make." He could feel the heat crawling up his neck to splash across his cheeks while she laughed. "You're blushing!"

"I am not."

"Yes, you are." She laid her hand across his for a moment and said, "I love a man who can blush. I think it's cute."

Pulling her hand back, she jumped up and moved toward the grill while the smell of barbeque wafted to his nose, making his mouth water. "Damn, those smell good."

"I'm a pretty good cook, if I do say so myself." She turned the meat again before closing the lid. "I'll be right back. Those are done. I just need to get the other stuff unless you'd rather eat in the house."

"Out here is fine. It's a pretty night, actually."

"All right. Why don't you get the steaks off the grill, and I'll make the plates?" Again, she disappeared into the house, returning a few moments later with two plates in her hands and placing them on the patio table.

He sat across the table from her, watching her delicate hands wield the steak knife while she cut the piece of meat on her plate. A soft sigh left her lips when she popped the steak into her mouth. He watched her lips, and his mouth wet dry as his cock hardened in his jeans, pressing firmly against the fly. Reaching for the beer, he took a long drink and tried desperately to calm the zing of desire rushing through him.

"Something wrong?"

"Huh—uh, no. It looks great." Pulling his gaze from her mouth, he tried to concentrate on the food in front of him.

* * * *

She sat back against the chair and lifted the beer to her lips. His gaze moved to her mouth, and his pupils dilated when she licked her lips, lapping up the drop of alcohol resting there.

Get a grip! The last thing I need is a temporary man in my life. He's only here for the weekend, but, oh, what a weekend it could be.

Sitting back up toward her plate, she continued to eat, steering the conversation to safer topics. "Is rodeo all you do for a living?"

A small grin lifted the corners of his mouth. "Why?"

"Just curious. Unless you are pro, it's hard to make a living that way."

"I'm a diesel mechanic, too."

"Like eighteen-wheelers?"

"Anything with a diesel engine. I've always been one to take things apart and put them back together again. It drove my parents crazy. During the summer, I do the rodeo thing mostly. In the winter, I work on trucks and break horses for Chase."

"I bet. You can make a pretty good living riding bulls if you're good. Just look at Ty Murray," she said with a chuckle.

"Yeah. I wish I was that good."

"Do your brothers raise horses or cows?"

"Justin runs cattle, but Chase and Abby bred quarter horses."

She dropped her fork when her startled look met his, and he frowned. "Something wrong?"

"You're a Wilder from the Rocking W?"

"Yeah, that's Chase's place, but it belonged to my parents before that. Why?"

"Shit!" She grabbed her plate and headed for the house.

Chapter Three

"Do you wanna tell me what's wrong?" He stood behind her, itching to touch her back where her hair lay against her shoulders.

She turned around. Her eyes masked against whatever thoughts ran through her mind. "I…um…I'm sorry, Cole. It's nothing really."

He frowned. "It didn't sound like nothing. You seemed shocked or surprised, like you knew my family."

She wouldn't look at him while she started fiddling with the sponge on the counter, wiping at some imaginary dirt. "No. What I mean is that I've heard of them. That's all. Your brother's reputation is well known amongst ranchers."

He took her chin in his hand, forcing her to bring her eyes back to his. "Why do I think there is more to this than you are saying?" *Damn, I want to kiss her. If her mouth tasted as good as it look, I'm a goner.*

Her eyes widened for a second before his gaze slid to her lips. They parted slightly on a soft sigh.

He let his fingers trail along her jaw while her tongue slipped out and she licked her lips. Sliding his hand around the back of her neck, he cupped her head. The need to taste her and to feel her against him overwhelmed him. Their breaths mixed in the air between them, and her eyes drifted shut.

"Carrie?"

She jumped, and her palms came up to push against his chest until he stepped back and dropped his hands.

"Jess?" Her voice sounded breathless, even to him.

"Where are you?"

"In the kitchen."

A young woman with hair a little lighter than Carrie's stopped in the doorway, and her eyes widened when she saw him standing next to her sister.

"Uh...sorry. I didn't realize you had company."

"It's fine. Jess, this is Cole. Cole, this is Jessica, my sister."

"Hi. It's nice to meet you."

Carrie's sister's gaze started at his face and wandered down his chest. She didn't bother to mask her interest in his groin before her gaze continued to the boots on his feet and then made its way back to his face. "Nice."

"Jessica!"

"What? I can't appreciate a nice looking guy?"

"That's what got you in the mess you're in. By the way, where in the hell were you?"

"Out." Jessica turned and headed toward the living room with Carrie hot on her heels while he followed.

"What do you mean out? You are seventeen, Jessica. You are supposed to be in the house when I get home from the store."

"I'm not a baby, Carrie. I'm almost eighteen, and I can go out with my friends if I want to."

By this time, the two women were toe-to-toe while Carrie tried to curb the younger woman's behavior. He grinned. Obviously it wasn't working too well from what he could tell.

"No, you are not a baby, but you aren't eighteen yet. Until then, you are my responsibility. You've gotten yourself into enough of a mess."

Jessica's eyes darted to him as he stood against the doorway.

"Don't worry about him. He knows all about your problem. He's Jimmy's friend and the man I accused of getting you pregnant last night at the bar."

"You what? Damn, Carrie. Now the whole damned town knows." Jess grumbled before she headed for the stairs. Jessica glanced at him before she took the stairs two at a time and then slammed the door to her room.

Carrie's shoulders slumped when the fight drained out of her and she walked back to the couch. She dropped onto the leather surface with a sigh.

He sat beside her and pulled her against his side. Why it felt so right to hold her, he wasn't sure.

She shook her head. "I don't know what I'm going to do with her."

"I'm sure your parents thought the same thing about you a few years ago." He chuckled.

Tilting her head up, she looked in his eyes. "I was never like that."

"Always the good girl?"

She dropped her gaze. "Well, maybe not always."

He laughed again. "I get the feeling you were a little more on the wild side yourself. More than you are willing to admit, too."

She pulled away. "I never snuck out or didn't come in before my curfew. My dad would have beaten my ass."

"Mmm…" His gaze drifted down when he thought about what he'd like to do with her ass, and a few well placed smacks might be interesting.

* * * *

"Stop looking at me like that." She stood up, walking toward the cold fireplace, rubbing her arms, trying desperately to calm the goose bumps flittering across the surface.

"Like what?"

"Like you would like to…" She shivered as her gaze met his again. The heat reflected there sent desire zinging along her nerve ends to settle in the pit of her stomach before it spread like wildfire to her groin. The promise his eyes had her pussy throbbing with need and her panties soaking wet.

"I *would* like to," he whispered loud enough she heard every word, every inflection of each syllable.

She shook her head in denial even if her body was screaming, *Yes, oh, yes.* "I'm not into temporary men, Cole. I've got a strict no touch policy on rodeo guys."

"I'm not expecting anything, Carrie. All I said was I would like to. Can't blame a guy for wanting to." He stretched his arm across the back of the couch while he watched her.

Damn, why does he have to be so gorgeous?

She lifted her shoulder in a shrug. "I guess not."

"Besides, you're a very desirable woman. I would have to be a complete fool if I said I didn't want you." His dimples creased his cheeks when he smiled. "I'm not a fool."

She inhaled sharply when his words reached her ears, and she could feel liquid seep between her legs again at just the thought. Shifting uncomfortably, she tried to relieve some of the pressure building between her thighs. "I'm sure you say that to all the girls."

A playboy smile graced his lips although he didn't comment on her observation. It wasn't like she wasn't attracted to him because that much was obvious, but she had enough of men who just wanted a short-term thing, a quick roll in the hay.

"Listen. We should probably call it a night. I appreciate all your help today."

His eyebrow rose at her tone and her words. "Dismissal—got it." Shuffling to his feet, he grabbed the standard black Stetson he wore all day and put it back on his head. "Thanks for dinner."

"No problem."

"I guess I'll see you around."

"Probably not. You'll be leaving in a day or so, and I'll be right here in Silver Ridge."

"True." He stopped in front of her, and she was afraid he would finish the kiss he started earlier, or afraid he wouldn't, she wasn't sure.

Lifting his hand, he trailed his fingers down her cheek. Her nipples hardened with just the thought of his callused palms sliding over the firm peaks of her breasts. He let his hand drop to his side and said, "Bye, Carrie."

She shuddered when he turned away and headed for the door. He shot a glance over his shoulder before he opened it and quickly walked outside, pulling it closed behind him.

* * * *

Dust rolled through the air when the horse and rider rode by when Carrie approached the rodeo participants parking area.

What in the hell am I doing here?

Her eyes traveled around the many cowboys and cowgirls lining the vicinity, searching for the one man she'd come to find. When he walked away last night, her whole body had been on high alert to his touch, his smell, and what his kiss would be like. Tossing and turning, she awoke this morning more sexually frustrated than she had been in years. After some deep soul searching and a phone call to her best friend, Katie, she decided to try to find him. She hated one night stands, and she hated short-term relationships, but for some reason she was fascinated by Cole Wilder.

Your mother would roll over in her grave if she knew you were even talking to a Wilder, much less spending time with one, her head screamed. Her heart skipped a beat when it whispered its own fevered wish—*Live your life, Carrie.*

She walked briskly along the metal fencing, her eyes darting back and forth, looking at each face. When she had almost made the complete circle of cowboys and cowgirls as well as the horse trailers, she found him sitting on the tailgate of his truck. His eyebrows rose in surprise when he saw her.

She shuffled toward him, embarrassed now that she searched him out.

"Hi," he said, slipping off the truck bed.

"Hi." Tearing her gaze away from his, she looked at the toes of her boots as she scuffed them in the dirt at her feet.

He cleared his throat. "The store closed today?"

She looked up. "Yeah. I always close it on Sunday."

"Did you come out to watch the competition?"

"In a way, I guess." She shrugged and her heart whispered, *Just say it, Carrie.* "I really came to find you."

"Really. Why?"

"To apologize for last night."

He smiled, flashing those devastating dimples in her direction, and she almost tripped over her boots.

"I'm sorry it sounded like I was dismissing you. In a way I was, I guess. It's like I said before, I have a no touch policy when it comes to rodeo guys."

His mouth turned down in a frown. "Then why are you here?"

"Because I was seriously contemplating rethinking my policy, at least for you."

"And?"

"I just thought we might be able to get to know each other a little better even though you are leaving tomorrow or the next day."

"What are you saying, Carrie?"

She huffed, planting her hands on her hips and said, "Do I have to spell it out for you?"

He smiled again, and her heart thumped in her chest. "Yeah, I guess you do."

Tipping her head back for a moment, she sighed and then looked at him again. She grumbled under her breath. *Difficult man.* Knowing he probably heard her by the widening of his grin, she tried desperately not to roll her eyes like a schoolgirl.

"I like you, Cole, and I thought maybe…" *This was stupid. I shouldn't have given into my lust and sought him out.* Losing her nerve she mumbled, "Never mind."

She turned her back, intending on stomping her way back to the spectator stands. He grabbed her hand and pulled her toward him, wrapping his arm around her waist. Her breath left her lungs in a whoosh when her breasts slammed against the rock hard expanse of his chest.

His voice dropped to a whisper when he stared into her eyes. "I like you, too, and I would love to get to know you better, but make no mistake, I'm not the settlin' kind."

She pushed at the hard muscles beneath her hands, but he wouldn't budge. "I'm not looking for a permanent fixture in my life, Cole. I've got enough problems keeping Jess out of trouble and making sure the store stays running to worry about a man."

He chuckled. "As long as we're on the same page, darlin'." His eyes swept her face and settled on her lips for a moment. A second later, he brushed them lightly with his before released her. "I need to go. I'm up in a bit."

"Uh…yeah…sure," she murmured and stepped back.

"Meet me back here after my ride. We'll see what kind of trouble we can find." There were those dimples again when his eyes sparkled in challenge.

Not waiting for her to reply, he grabbed his hat and rope before he headed for the arena. She watched his nicely emphasized ass in his tight Wranglers and muscular thighs encased in smooth chaps. He made her squirm with his good looks and luscious body, and she felt her face flush with embarrassment. Looking around quickly to see if anyone saw her, she ducked her head and headed for the stands.

Finding a seat down in the front, she could see him laughing with a couple of other riders while they stood behind the shoot waiting their turn. Two riders later and it was his turn. He climbed up on the metal fence where the bull shifted, pushing against the confines of the small area. Climbing over the top, he settled on the back of the huge animal and secured the bull rope around his gloved hand. She held her breath as she waited for him to give the signal he was ready.

After a brief nod of his head, the gate shot open, and the bull charged out several feet before his hind legs shot out behind him. Her heart clenched while she watched, terrified he would be hurt. For what seemed like hours, his right hand whipped through the air, back and forth, and the bull twisted and turned almost as if it were trying to dislodge a fly.

The buzzer finally rang loud and clear, and the crowd erupted in a loud cheer. Cole managed to get his hand free and jump away from the bull while the clowns did their job, distracting the enraged animal before it could gore someone. He flashed his dimpled smile and waved to the crowd before leaping onto the fence and slinging his leg over, dropping to his feet on the other side.

She stood, trying to be nonchalant while she walked headed for the stairs to meet him at his truck, her heart pounding. She let her mind wander slightly while she imaged what the coming afternoon and evening would present. When she rounded the horse trailers, she could see the side of his big black Ford, and she smiled when she headed for the tailgate.

The sight that met her eyes dropped her heart to her toes.

Chapter Four

Jumping down from the fence after his ride, his heart pounded while the full force of adrenaline rushed through him. Blood swirled through his veins, almost giving him an erection from the excitement. His penis pushed insistently upward, and he thought with a chuckle, Down boy!

A large smile was plastered on his face while he endured the slaps of congratulations from his competitors before he headed back for his truck.

His thoughts turned toward Carrie, and excitement zinged through him. He couldn't believe how pumped he was thinking about the coming night and spending some time wooing the reluctant hazel-eyed beauty into his bed. To be near her, to hold her, touch her, seeing if the inside of her mouth tasted as sweet as her lips did, had him almost running back in the direction of his truck.

Stopping at the tailgate, disappointment rippled along his arms when he noticed she wasn't there. He shrugged and unbuckled his chaps around his waist before he bent over to unzip them at the sides. The next thing he felt was a warm hand sliding over his ass cheeks. Assuming the hand belonged to Carrie, he stood up slowly, only to meet the bright blue eyes of voluptuous platinum blonde.

"Hey, sugar," she whispered while her hands slid around him and she squashed her breasts against his chest. "How about you let me ride you like you just rode that bull?" Before he could even utter a word, she wrapped one hand around the back of his head and planted her collagen-filled red lips against his. Never one to deny himself the kiss of a pretty woman, he lost himself in her touch.

A startled gasp caught his attention and he pulled away. The first thing he saw was Carrie's wide hazel eyes when she took in the scene. Pushing against the strange woman until she released him, he hurried around the side of the truck, but in the blink of an eye, Carrie was gone, disappearing between the vehicles. He tried to follow, calling her name, but the other woman grabbed a hold of his arm.

Shaking her off angrily, he followed in the direction Carrie disappeared, but the only thing he saw was the dust left in the air as her truck pulled out onto the highway. Debating whether to follow her, he walked back toward his truck only to find the blonde perched on the tailgate.

"So what do you say we hook up?"

Shooting her an angry stare, he growled. "Beat it. Go find some other pretty boy to spend your night with. I'm not interested."

The woman huffed and fumed. "I never!"

"I doubt that," he spat and she spun on her heels and stomped away.

Running his hands through his hair, he tried to decide whether to go after Carrie or not. He could find his way back to her place, but as mad as she probably was, she wouldn't see him.

"Damn it!" Slamming his hand against the side of his truck, he shook it for a moment when pain shot up his arm. He grabbed his gear and whipped open the door before he slid inside.

Two hours later found him at the bar where he first met her, nursing a beer with Jimmy sitting next to him. His hand hurt like hell, but it couldn't dull the pain that centered in his chest somewhere above his heart.

"What's in your craw, Cole? You've been grumbling for the last couple of hours."

"Nothin'."

"Yeah right! I saw you brush off the blonde babe at the rodeo. She was hot for you, man, and you walked away. That ain't like you."

His gaze scanned the crowd, hoping she would be here but knowing she probably wouldn't. He couldn't blame her, really. He had made sure she knew he wanted to be with her tonight, and then she came back to find him making out with someone else.

What else would she think after catching me playing tonsil hockey with another woman? Hell, I think I'm an ass. I can imagine what she thinks.

"Like I said, it's nothin', Jim. Just forget it."

"Well, I think I'm gonna find me a pretty babe to dance with. Your company sucks, buddy." The other man moved away from his side and headed for a group of women standing off to the side of the bar. Several of them had been trying to get his attention for the last thirty minutes, but he wasn't interested. One hazel-eyed beauty had him tied up in knots.

Taking a long drink of the beer in his hand, he shook his head. *Why in the hell am I sitting here by myself with all these pretty women around? Maybe I need to hook up with one and forget about the little tigress.*

Feeling a warm hand on his shoulder, he looked in the mirror over the bar and was startled to see who stood next to him.

"Carrie?"

"Hi." She let her hand drop as he spun around on the stool.

"What are you doing here? I didn't figure you would even want to be in the same room with me after what happened at the rodeo."

She dropped her gaze to the floor. "Well, I thought I should at least give you the chance to explain."

Taking her hand in his, he entwined their fingers. "I didn't even know her. She was just there when I went back to my truck after the ride."

"A rodeo whore?"

"Something like that, yeah."

She shrugged, but still wouldn't meet his gaze until he put his fingers under her chin and forced her to look up.

"It doesn't really matter, Cole. I mean, we both know there isn't anything between us. Tonight was just supposed to be a good time, right?"

"Uh…yeah." Somehow hearing her put it that way didn't sit well with him.

"Well, then, let's have a good time." She backed up, pulling him with her onto the dance floor. Slipping her hands up around his neck, he settled his own on her hips and pulled her close.

The sweet scent of roses met his nose, wrapping around his senses when he inhaled. Her breasts pressed against his chest, and desire started building in his veins. Sliding his cheek along hers, he could feel her soft hair brushing his face. His hands tightened on her waist before they slid around her back to pull her in tighter. God, she felt perfect in his arms.

Her breathing quickened when they moved together to the sway of the music. He wanted to let his hands drift down to her ass cheeks so bad his palms itched, but he wouldn't embarrass her like that. She probably knew most of the people in this bar, grew up with them, and he didn't want anyone to think she was easy or a *rodeo whore* as she had put it.

The music stopped, and they both sighed before they stepped apart. He took her hand and headed back to the bar. Finding the same stool, he perched on it and pulled her up next to him while she slid her arm around his shoulder and his hand rested on her waist.

"What would you like to drink?"

"Beer is fine."

"So where is Jess tonight?"

She frowned while her gaze swept the bar. "I don't know. She's being so difficult. She won't tell me where she's going or what she's doing. The only thing I do know is that she's not here."

"You can't fix everything, Carrie. She's almost old enough to make her own decisions."

A sigh rushed from between her lips. "I know, but I just wish she would think about things before she does them. Just like getting pregnant. She obviously didn't think it through when she slept with your friend a couple of months ago."

He cocked an eyebrow in her direction while he wondered what it would take to make her lose control, throw caution to the wind and go to bed with him. "Sometimes thinking isn't part of the equation."

"Well, it should be. With as much birth control and stuff that's available now, getting pregnant when you don't want to shouldn't be happening."

He leaned over, pushing her hair away from her ear when he nuzzled it with his nose, and his hand caressed her hip. "Haven't you ever lost control? Just did something you know you shouldn't have because it felt good?"

"I…uh…"

Pulling back with a devilish grin, he said, "We'll have to explore that."

* * * *

Damn, the man can turn my insides to mush with nothing more than a whisper. What was I thinking coming here? She took a long drink of the beer in her hand. You are in way over your head, Carrie, her head whispered.

A man hopped up on the stage when the band took a break. "Hey y'all. Someone wants to make an announcement. Come on up here, Joey."

"Shit," she grumbled and pulled away from Cole side.

"Carrie, sweetie. Come here, honey."

She shook her head, and she felt Cole stiffen beside her.

"Come on, baby. We need to make this official," Joey coaxed from the stage.

Anger reverberated through her as she stomped toward the platform. "Get down, Joey."

"Nope." His drunken stare turned from her and she sighed, rolling her eyes to the ceiling. "Hey, everybody. Carrie and I are gettin' married."

Applause resounded through the crowd mixed with laughter, and she tried to grab the man's hand and pull him down from the stage. He held on, tugging her up with him and wrapping his arm around her waist. She pushed him away and headed for the edge of the plywood, but when she lifted her gaze to the bar where Cole had been standing, he was gone.

She searched the crowd until she finally caught sight of him when he reached the door. He turned and looked back a moment before he pushed through the doorway and the wood panel slammed shut behind him.

Jumping down, she dove through the throng of people until she reached the outside door. She saw him just as he reached his truck. He stopped and braced his hands against the bed, giving her enough time to reach his side.

"Cole."

He spun around, anger bright in his eyes. "You could have told me, Carrie."

"There isn't anything to tell."

"Are you trying to say that guy didn't ask you to marry him?"

"No, that's not what I'm saying."

"I don't mess with married women," he growled before he pulled the door open.

She grabbed his arm before he could get inside and slam the door. "I'm not married, never have been, and I'm not going to be any time soon that I'm aware of."

"He said you were gettin' married."

"Joey has been my friend since I was a baby. He's been askin' me to marry him for the last five years. Didn't you see everyone laughing? Everybody who lives around here knows it's almost a joke, and they know it ain't happenin'."

"You aren't gettin' married?"

"No."

His arm snaked around her waist so fast she didn't have a chance to react, before his mouth swooped down on hers. He stole her breath away and gave it back mixed with his. Slanting his lips across hers, he traced the crease with his tongue, asking for permission to explore inside her mouth. She whimpered and opened to him as his tongue slid inside and stroked hers. He pulled her closer, fitting her to his hard frame, breasts to hard chest, belly to belly, thigh to thigh until he slipped one of his muscled legs between hers. His hands cupped her ass, lifting her tighter against him while he moaned low in his throat, and she could feel his hard length between them.

With a tortured groan, he pulled his mouth away, and she tipped her head to the side, giving him access to her neck while her hands held on to his shoulders. He nipped at the soft skin with his teeth before soothing it with his tongue, and shivers rolled down her back.

"God, Carrie," he growled, lifting his head. "If we don't stop this, I'm taking you back to your house and fuck you right now."

She felt her body come alive at his words. Mind warred with body. Wanting him more than she'd ever wanted someone before had her throwing caution to the wind.

I'll explain to Jess later, if she finds out. It's been too damned long since I've been with a man, and I need this one.

Her labia pulsed and filled. Her clit rubbing against her panties was almost enough to send her into oblivion, but she wanted him to come along, too. "So what's stopping you, cowboy?"

Chapter Five

Their eyes met. His held a question, hers the answer. *Am I really going to let him make love to me?* Her heart whispered with a resounding, *Yes.*

"Get in the truck." He let her go, almost pushing her inside the cab before he slid in beside her. Sexual tension filled the air, crackling between them when they ripped out of the parking lot, spraying gravel before finding pavement.

They didn't speak on the short ride back to her house. She didn't know what to say. She had never wanted something so badly in her life as she wanted to feel this man wrapped around her, holding her and making her body come alive with his. Instinctively knowing what was about to happen between them would be earth shattering to say the least, she laid her palm on his thigh and smiled when the muscle tensed beneath her touch.

He pulled the truck into her driveway, popping the door open in his haste before the engine even stopped. Her feet touched the hard surface of the concrete, and he grasped her hand before they headed for the door. She moaned softly when she felt his lips on her shoulder, nibbling at the tender skin. Her hands shaking, she slipped the key in the lock before she pushed the door open. He followed her inside, and she no more than got the door shut behind them when he had her up against the hard surface, his hands on either side of her shoulders.

His lips were only a breath away when he whispered, "Are you sure about this?"

He was giving her a chance to retreat—save face if she so chose, but she had craved his touch from the moment he stayed at the store to help her. She wasn't going to let him walk away without at least sampling what he had to offer.

"Carrie?" His warm breath caressed her lips as his eyes searched hers.

"I'm very sure."

Her heart thumped in her chest, slamming against her ribs when that sexy-as-hell smile rippled across his mouth, showing off the dimples in his cheeks.

Good God, I love those dimples!

"Where's your room?" His lips flittered against her cheek, moving along softly until he found her ear, and she shuddered before she answered in a breathless whisper.

"Up the stairs, first door on the left."

He bent down and scooped her up in his arms, taking the stairs two at the time in his haste as she felt a giggle rise in her chest. Pushing the door shut with his foot, he moved toward the bed but stopped at the side before he lowered her to her feet.

She peeked at him through her lashes before she reached her shaking hands toward his chest. Unbuttoning his shirt, she slowly revealed his sculpted muscles, and her mouth water to taste him. The spatter of chest hair sent heat straight to her center when her lips found his skin, and he groaned at her touch. His hands moved softly up and down her arms while she continued to play across the expanse of his chest with her lips. When she found the flat disk of his male nipple, she caressed it with her tongue, then nibbled with her teeth. His hiss, followed by the quiver of his skin, made her smile. Slipping the shirt from his shoulders and letting it fall to the floor at their feet, she reached for the belt buckle at his waist, but he stopped her. Her eyes swept up to meet his heated gaze.

"My turn."

His kiss started at her forehead before it moved along her cheek, across her nose, and back to her mouth. He pulled her tight to his chest, and she could feel the hard muscles pressed intimately against her breasts. Running his tongue along the crease of her lips, she opened them for him, letting him stroke the inside of her mouth. His hand slipped up her side to underneath her breast, his thumb caressing the nipple through her shirt. His mouth moved across her cheek to her ear, tugging and nipping at her soft earlobe before sliding down her neck.

"Your skin is so soft," he whispered, trailing his tongue and lips to her shoulder as his fingers worked the tank top up her chest. He released her long enough to pull the shirt and her bra over her head and drop them to the floor.

She let her hands wander down his back, scratching slightly, smoothing the muscles that bunched and rolled beneath her fingers. Coming back to his chest, she stroked the fine hair beneath her touch and she smiled when she heard a growl.

Trailing a hot, wet kiss down her chest, he found the taut nipple with his mouth, sucking until it hardened to an aching point. She shivered when goose bumps rose across her skin, and a soft moan escaped her lips. His hands worked the button loose at her waist, sliding inside the waistband and working the jeans down her thighs. Finding her ass cheeks with both hands, he kneaded her soft flesh, molding it to his touch. He pulled her so her hips were flush against him before his lips found hers again in a desperate kiss.

She worked her jeans off, stepping out of them, before she went for the buckle at his waist. Undoing it and the button quickly, she slipped her hands inside his boxers, stroking his hard length as he growled into her mouth.

Stepping back with a saucy smile, she dropped to her knees. One hand cupped his balls while her tongue darted out, licking the pre-cum from the tip. His hands twisted in her hair, holding her head in place. She flicked her tongue over the tip and smiled when she heard a hiss above her. Stroking his cock from base to tip, she moved down and took his entire length inside her mouth until the tip bumped the back of her throat. His thighs quivered when she slowly moved back to the tip, and he groaned above her. Her fingers caressed the sack at the base, moving between his balls to the small area of soft skin that joined them with his ass.

He let her play for several minutes before a tortured growl ripped from his lips and he pulled her back up in front of him. His mouth dove for hers, taking her lips in a frantic kiss as he pushed her back toward the bed. She felt the mattress on the back of her knees before he laid her down and moved over her.

The coarse hair rubbing along hers sent her nerve endings on high alert. His mouth left hers to nibble at the corners of her lips before moving to her ear and tracing the outline. He continued his journey to the soft spot below her ear, stopping to bite lightly before soothing the sting with his tongue.

She arched her back as his hand found her breast, kneading the soft flesh. Her nipple hardened beneath his palm while he molded it to his touch. His thumb flicked the nipple before rolling it softly between his forefinger and thumb while she gasped and pressed deeper in his touch. His mouth moved down her chest and took the hard bud between his lips, sucking hard, sending electricity straight to her wet pussy.

His callused palm slipped across her stomach and toward the spot between her legs aching for his touch. When he reached for her, she shifted and opened for him, but he avoided touching where she ached to have him the most. Instead, his hand moved down her thigh and back up the inside. She held her breath, waiting, throbbing. As she felt his fingers whisper against her labia, she groaned low in her throat, and he smiled against her skin.

"God—Cole, please. Touch me."

She moaned and tossed her head when he spread her with his fingers before his thumb rasped against her clit. He continued to pleasure her while his mouth licked and suckled at her breast. The sensations he caused with his touch drove her to the edge of satisfaction.

A moment later, he settled between her legs, and his tongue lapped at her center. Heat curled from her toes and up her legs until she arched against him and cried out his name.

Coming down from her ecstasy, it took her a minute to focus on his face when he moved up and kissed across her cheek. His rock hard erection pressed against her hip, and she moved her hand to grasp him, encircling his girth while he moaned deep in his throat.

"Be careful. That thing is loaded."

"I'm counting on it," she whispered and shifted onto her side and captured his lips with hers. Their tongues danced together for several moments before she broke the kiss and met his gaze. "Do you have a condom?"

His finger drifted down her cheek and he murmured, "Yeah." He reached for his pants and pulled out his wallet. A sexy grin appeared on his mouth when he held up the foil packet before he ripped it open.

He slipped the condom over his shaft while she watched with rapt attention. She had never watched a guy put on a condom before, but the whole thing was totally arousing when it was Cole.

Moving back to her side, he kissed her again, sliding his tongue inside her mouth, stroking the inside softly as she moaned beneath him. His thumb stroked her nipple, bringing the nub to a hard point before his mouth trailed down her chest to take it between his lips.

"God, Cole—please."

He lifted his head and flashed his dimples. "Please what?"

"I want you inside me," she whispered, embarrassed at the desperation in her voice. She knew she had never wanted anyone as much as she wanted him right this moment, right now.

He moved over the top of her, slipping his hips between her thighs, and she groaned softly at the feel of his cock pressed against her belly. She brought her legs up around his hips, arching her pelvis and begging him with her eyes.

With a moan, he shifted, pressing the tip of his cock against her. He rocked forward, pushing inside her slightly before pulling back.

Her breath hitched in her throat, and she ran her fingernails down his back while she shifted, wanting him deeper. His eyes closed tightly, and his jaw appeared clamped hard, making his cheek tick as he fought for control. When he lifted her hips, she nipped at his chest with her teeth. A tortured growl ripped from his lips, and he plunged forward, driving his cock inside her until he was fully seated.

He didn't move for a moment. "God, you feel good," he murmured.

She whimpered, desperate for him to move and take her over the edge. When he shifted his hips, pulling back before plunging again, she thought she had died and gone to heaven. The friction of his cock inside her was driving her crazy, but when he lifted his chest and pulled her legs up so her calves were across his biceps, she almost squealed in delight.

The slap of flesh against flesh was loud in the room while her sighs and his growls of pleasure mixed together. Her climax hit her almost out of nowhere. Stars burst behind her eyelids, and she arched her back before she screamed his name. He pounded his pelvis against hers several more times before he groaned his own completion.

He let her legs slip down around his hips again before he braced his arms on either side of her shoulders while they tried to catch their breath. They both moaned when he slipped from her warmth and rolled onto the bed next to her. He brought her against his side and she reached down to the end of the bed to pull the sheet over the top of them. She snuggled next to his warmth and sighed.

Before she had a chance to react, the door to her room creaked open, and Jessica poked her head through the opening. "Carrie?" Jessica's wide eyes met hers as she sat up in the bed. "Oh my God! I don't believe you!"

"Jess, let me explain." She reached down and grabbed her shirt and jeans from the floor.

"Explain what, Carrie?" The angry, accusing stare Jessica shot her sent her heart to her toes. "You are such a hypocritical bitch!" Jessica whipped around and practically ran down the hall to her own room.

"Jessica!" She quickly slipped her shirt on and yelled again, "Jessica!"

When Carrie's clothing was in some semblance of order, she quickly headed down the hall after her sister. She tried turning the handle on her sister's bedroom door, but it was locked. "Jessica, open this door."

"Leave me alone!"

"Jess, let me explain."

"There isn't anything to explain, Carrie. You've known that guy for what—two days and you obviously fucked him tonight. Yet you give me the fucking third degree over sleeping with a guy and getting pregnant."

"Jessica Anne! You will not use that language with me."

"Go to hell, Carrie!"

Carrie took a deep breath, trying to calm the anger and humiliation she felt before she tried again. "Jessie, open the door so we can talk."

Silence met her ears, and she knocked again. "Come on, Jess, open the door." Still nothing. "I'm sorry. I know I can't judge you now for what happened." Silence. "Yes, I'm a hypocrite. I threw caution to the wind and had sex with a man I just met. Big difference here, little sister. I'm twenty-six years old and you aren't even eighteen. I can take responsibility for my actions. You can't at seventeen, but I'm sorry and I was wrong."

She waited a few moments before she turned around and headed back for her room. Her gaze met Cole's where he stood at the door, leaning against the doorframe. His clothing was now in place, covering the broad, muscled expanse of his chest, much to her disappointment.

"I'm sorry," she whispered when she reached his side.

"Don't be." He lifted his hand to lightly brush his fingers across her lips. A shiver ran down her back.

"You probably should go."

"Yeah. I know." A wry smile crossed his lips. "One problem, though."

"What's that?"

"Your truck is still at the bar."

"Shit! I forgot."

"Let me run you over there at least so you can pick it up, since our plans have obviously been waylaid."

Our plans. It's strange to think of it like that, but I guess it was our plans. She stepped back, and he dropped his hand. "I would appreciate the lift."

Distance. She needed to put distance between them. His touch was too intoxicating, and if she spent much more time in his arms, she would give in to the desire rushing through her veins like the rapids on the Colorado River. She wanted his touch, needed it desperately, but her senses returned, and she realized the mistake she just made.

The ride back to the bar was uncomfortable. He didn't talk, and she felt too foolish for what happened to say anything. Parking next to her vehicle, he slipped his into park and shut off the engine. His gaze focused on something outside the window as if he didn't want to look at her at all, and her heart clenched.

The bar was still in full swing, the music loud even where they sat, and she wondered if he would go back inside once she left. The thought disturbed her somehow.

He sighed before he opened his door, walked around to the passenger side, and pulled her door open.

"Cole…"

"Carrie…"

They both laughed.

"You go first."

"No. Ladies first."

Chewing her bottom lip nervously, she focused on the toes of her boots for a second before she started to apologize again.

"Carrie, it's fine, really."

She shook her head. "No, it's not, Cole. I probably shouldn't have let things happen the way they did. I've always prided myself on control."

"Are you sorry we made love?"

"No—yes. I don't know. Being near you confuses me."

"I see." He frowned and stepped back further.

"What I mean is I made a mistake tonight. It's been a long time since a man has held me, and I guess I just gave into the temptation of having you here. I've been under so much pressure with quitting school, dealing with taking care of Jessica, and now her pregnancy...I needed someone. That's why I dismissed the fact that you are only here temporarily." She moved away, her back to him as she let her head drop against her shoulder and sighed.

He stopped behind her and pulled her back into his embrace. She leaned back, letting his heat envelope her while his hands moved down her arms.

"And because we're attracted to each other." His whispered words caressed her ear, and shivers rolled down her spine.

"Yeah, but that doesn't make it right."

"Sometimes you have to grab on to something as it happens."

"I can't keep throwing caution to the wind, Cole." She turned back around to face him. "It's not right for me to be judgmental of her."

"She made that mistake on her own a couple of months ago."

"Yes, she did, and I made the same mistake." She shivered when his fingers moved down her neck, and she closed her eyes.

Good Lord, what his touch does to me.

"I don't think what happened between us was a mistake," he whispered against her lips.

Her eyes opened slightly. "Maybe not a mistake, but definitely an error in judgment."

He lifted his head but didn't let her go. "You're a grown woman. She's still a kid."

"I should have known better. I need to set an example…"

He pressed a finger to her lips to silence her and looked deep into her eyes. "There isn't anything wrong with wanting to make love with someone just because."

She removed his finger and stepped away. "It wasn't making love Cole. It was sex—pure and simple."

"I'm not going to win this argument am I?" He smiled, flashing those devastatingly handsome dimples.

She chuckled slightly and shook her head.

He pulled her against his chest, and she wrapped her arms around his waist, laying her head on his shoulder. For several moments, he held her, stroked her back and she knew it was a moment she would never forget. Sighing heavily, she finally moved out of his embrace.

"I should go."

"I know," he whispered, tugging on her hand gently to bring her back into his arms "Let me take you to dinner tomorrow."

"Aren't you leaving?"

"Not tomorrow. I'm riding again during the day. We hadn't planned on leaving until the day after."

God, I want to. I want to see him again, I want him to hold me, kiss me and make love to me, even if it's the wrong thing to do.

She closed her eyes as his fingers moved to the hair by her ear and around to the back of her head. His lips played softly along the seam of hers, nibbling at the corners of her mouth, before his tongue coaxed her to open for him. With a tortured groan, he slanted his mouth across hers, taking everything she offered and then some. He pushed her up against the truck, letting one hand wander down her side to cup her breast, his thumb working the nipple through her shirt. He finally lifted his mouth but continued to trail kisses along her cheek and down her neck, nipping softly.

When he finally lifted his head, they were both breathing hard. "Go out with me tomorrow."

I need to talk to Jess. If I get more involved with him without explaining things to her, she'll never understand. But I can't seem to tell him no.

His words weren't a question, they were a demand—one she would give in to willingly in her need to be near him. "Pick me up at the store at six."

A small grin rippled across his mouth. "Gladly." He trailed his fingers down her arm while goose bumps rose along her flesh behind them. "I'll see you then."

She sighed as he stepped back, and she walked around his truck to reach her own. Slipping inside the cab, she pulled the door shut and a shiver rolled down her back. Backing out of the parking stall, she waved and gave him a small smile before she pulled out onto the road headed for home. She looked in her rearview mirror and was happy to see him get back inside his own truck and start it, leaving the bar behind.

Chapter Six

Carrie rolled out of bed feeling more alive than she had in months. As her feet hit the floor, the soreness between her legs caught her a little off guard. She hadn't been with a man in over a year, and her body made sure she was aware of the fact. Grabbing a quick shower, she twisted her hair into a ponytail, slipped on her clothes, and padded down the stairs toward the kitchen. A quick cup of coffee, some toast, and she'd be ready to face the day. She stopped short when her gaze found Jessica sitting at the table nibbling on some toast.

She moved toward her sister, wrapped her arms around her shoulders, and gave her a hug. "I'm sorry about last night, Jess."

Jessica shrugged, but tears sparkled on her lashes when Carrie stepped back and took the seat beside her. "I never should have judged you. I've made mistakes myself in life, and it's not fair for me to say anything. I really wish you would have thought things through a little before you slept with Jimmy, but it's over and done now." She put her hand on her sister's stomach. "You're gonna have a baby, and we just have to move forward and deal with it."

Jessica leaned over and hugged Carrie, sniffing and wiping her tears. "I'm sorry, too. I shouldn't have said those things last night. You haven't even been on a date since you came home from school, much less had a chance to meet anyone and have a relationship."

Carrie dropped her gaze. She didn't want her to see what was probably written all over her face.

"I guess you kinda like him, huh?"

"Yeah, but let's not talk about Cole, okay? I need to get some coffee and a quick bite before I head to the store." She rose to her feet and moved toward the pot on the counter.

"Can I ask you a question, Carrie?"

"Sure."

"You weren't a virgin last night, were you?"

Carrie closed her eyes and bit her lip. She needed to be honest with her sister, but it was a little difficult to talk about where and to whom she lost her virginity.

"No—no I wasn't, Jess."

"So when did you?"

She sighed before she turned and faced the quizzical expression on Jessica's face. "When I was sixteen. Remember Dustin?"

"Wasn't he the guy you were dating when you were a sophomore? The football player?"

"Yes."

"You lost it to him? Good lord, Carrie. He wasn't even half as cute as the guy you were with last night."

Carrie's gaze dropped to the table before she sat down. *No, Cole is the most gorgeous guy I've ever met, much less made love with.* "It doesn't matter."

"So what's between you and Cole? I thought you had a policy about rodeo guys."

"I do, and what's between Cole and I is none of your business." Taking the last sips of her coffee, she headed back into the kitchen before she left her cup in the sink. "You need to come to the store about eleven. It gets really busy then, and I need your help today."

Jessica huffed. "All right. I'll be there."

Carrie kissed her on the cheek, grabbed her keys, and walked out the door.

When she pulled into the store parking lot, she let a small, wistful smile lift the corners her mouth when she saw a very familiar black Ford. She grabbed her purse and keys before she slipped out, shut the door, and headed for the front of the store. As she slipped the key into the lock to unlock the door, she felt a warm breath against her ear. She shivered when Cole's hand came up to rest at her waist.

"Mmm...you smell good."

"What are you doing here?" She leaned back against his chest for a moment.

"I thought I'd come by and help for a little while," he whispered, his lips nibbling at her ear.

She pulled away and turned around, flashing him a smile. "I can always use cheap help."

"Cheap? I'll have you know, ma'am, I'm very expensive."

She cocked her head to the side as her eyes roamed over his chest, down his lean hips to his boots and back again. "I'm not sure I can afford you then."

A slow, sexy-as-hell grin spread across his face, showing off his dimples, and her heart skipped a beat. "I'm sure we can negotiate something."

They moved inside the store. She went and grabbed the cash bag before she walked back to the register. The bell over the door tinkled, announcing the arrival of a customer.

"Carrie?"

She groaned, and Cole frowned when Ken walked up to the counter.

"What can I get for you, Ken?"

His gaze ricocheted from her to Cole, who stood not far behind her, and then back to her. "Who's he?"

"None of your business. Is there something you need?"

"You know what I need."

"That's not happening, Ken, so forget it. If that's all you came in for, you can leave now."

* * * *

He didn't like the man. Something about him rubbed Cole the wrong way. Maybe it was his beady eyes. Maybe it was the possessive way he looked at Carrie. Whatever it was, the man brought out a protective side of his nature he didn't know he possessed. Stepping closer to Carrie, he laid his hand on her waist.

"Somethin' I can help you with, mister?"

Ken's eyes narrowed. "Some other time." He turned his back and walked out.

Carrie shivered and closed her eyes.

He pressed his lips to her temple and whispered, "You okay?"

She nodded and stepped out of his reach. He didn't like how she pulled away from him after their encounter with the other man.

The bell tinkled again and several customers came in. The two of them went back to the routine they had on Saturday with him filling orders and her ringing the purchases up until eleven rolled around.

Jessica walked in precisely on time, and he wasn't sure, but he thought he saw Carrie physically relax. They hadn't had a chance to talk at all since earlier that morning, and he wished he had time now, but he didn't. He had to ride in an hour.

"Hi. Cole, isn't it?"

"Yeah. How are you feeling?"

She dropped her eyes. "Fine."

"Can I talk to you a minute?"

Her gaze came back up to his, and she shrugged before she moved toward a corner of the store while Carrie was busy. She looked at him questioningly when they stopped near the back wall of the store.

"About last night..."

"It's okay. Carrie and I talked this morning."

"I just don't want you to think your sister goes around sleeping with guys she just met all the time."

She cocked at eyebrow at him and waited for him to explain.

"What I mean is—what happened between me and Carrie wasn't planned."

"I think that was obvious since, until three days ago, she didn't know who you were."

He shuffled his feet. *Damn! She's making me feel like the teenager here.*

"I don't begrudge Carrie anything. She gave up a lot when our parents died. Her dream was to have a career, not babysit her little sister, but she did it without complaining. She took over running this store to pay the bills, never once thinking about what it meant or how her life would change. Don't get me wrong, she has plenty of guys in this town who would love to catch her and hold on tight, but she's never been interested in anyone. Not until you came along."

"I—uh…"

She brought her finger up and poked him in the chest. "Don't hurt her, or you'll have me to deal with."

He smiled. "I'll try my best not to."

"See that you don't, cowboy." She turned to leave, but swung back around for a moment. "By the way, tell Jimmy I need to see him. He's got a responsibility he needs to take care of one way or another."

He watched her walk back to the cash register and take her place behind it without a backward glance in his direction. The flow of customers slowed down for the moment, and he moved to where Carrie stood stocking a shelf. He stopped at her side, and she looked up. "I need to go. I'm riding in a little bit."

"Thanks for your help this morning. You came to my rescue again." She stood and brushed the dirt on her hands across the thigh of her jeans.

He didn't know whether she was talking about the business or the asshole that had been harassing her this morning. "No problem. Are we still on for later?"

"Of course." She frowned. "That is unless you've changed your mind."

"Not on your life, lady. I'm looking forward to getting you alone again." Picking up a strand of hair lying on her shoulder, he ran his thumb over the end in a caress. She closed her eyes, and he bent his head, softly taking her lips with his in a light kiss. The kiss was meant to remind her of what they already shared, and when she shivered, he knew she remembered, just like he did. He wanted her on fire when they met later. The night before just made him want her more, and what he told her was the complete truth. He wanted her alone, lying beneath him, screaming his name when she came around him.

"I'll see you at six." He dropped a peck of a kiss on the end of her nose.

"Okay," she whispered when he stepped back.

He turned and headed for the door, but stopped when he reached it so he could see her one last time before he left. He flashed his best grin and winked, almost laughing out loud when she blushed.

* * * *

She sighed when he left before she turned back to stocking the shelf.

There's too much to do today to spend it daydreaming about Cole.

Her lips still tingled from the pressure of his.

Catching Jessica's knowing smile from near the register, she grumbled to herself and went back to work.

The rest of the day went by fairly quickly. Some of the rodeo participants came in, buying up some of her merchandise, feed, and tack broken during competition and needed replacing. Some even bought souvenirs from their little town.

When the clock struck five, Carrie walked the last few customers to the door, thanking them prior to locking it behind them. Before she could get it closed, someone pushed against the solid surface, throwing her aside as he rushed in, a mask over his face and a gun in his hand.

Jessica screamed, and the man waved the gun in her direction yelling, "Shut up, bitch!"

He turned toward Carrie. "Shut the door, lock it, and get over there by her."

Doing what she was told, she moved toward her sister and wrapped an arm around her shoulders while Jessica shook in her embrace.

"I want the money in the register."

She stiffened her shoulders and growled right back at him. "Get it yourself. I'm not helping you rob us."

"Don't tempt me, bitch, or I'll blow your brains all over the wall."

Jessica whimpered.

"Sshh. It'll be okay," Carrie whispered.

The masked man yanked the cash drawer off the counter, pulling the electrical cord right out of the wall, before shooting the register. He obviously didn't care of someone heard the gunshots or not.

Carrie smiled to herself, remembering the electronic alarm her father installed connected directly to the register. If the power were cut to it, the phone line would automatically dial the sheriff's department, sounding a silent burglar alarm. Within moments, the local police would have the place surrounded.

As sirens started blaring in the distance, panic registered in the man's eyes before he snarled and grabbed Carrie by the hair, pulling her away from Jessica. "You set off the fucking alarm!"

She glared right back. "You did it, not me. The register is rigged to dial when the power is cut off."

The man growled, pulled back his hand and slapped her hard across the face. Carrie reeled from the blow and slumped against the glass counter. She tried to stand up, but he grabbed her ponytail and yanked her up against him.

"We're leavin' here—together."

Wrapping his arm around her throat, he pushed the gun against her side when they walked toward the door. "Unlock the door."

With one hand on his arm trying to keep him from choking her, she reached with the other one to slide the bolt open. They walked out into the parking lot, only to see ten police cars, lights flashing, surrounding the store.

Chapter Seven

The rodeo events were in full swing. The bull riding was the biggest event of all and drew the most spectators to the arena. Cole looked over the crowd almost hoping to see Carrie among the sea of faces, but in his heart, he knew she wasn't there. The store didn't close until five, and he was to meet her there at six. There would be no reason for her to be at the arena unless she came to watch him. He smiled at the thought.

He stood next to the gate, getting ready for his final ride. Glove on, his bull rope in his hand, he hopped up on the metal railing, straddling it when he heard the crackle of a radio.

"Robbery in progress. All units respond code three—Marsh's Feed."

He felt the color drain from his face before he jumped down and grabbed the arm of the cop attached to the radio. The man glared at his hand before his gaze ricocheted back to Cole's face.

"I know you ain't grabbin' my arm there, cowboy."

"Sorry. Did they say robbery at Marsh's Feed?"

"Yeah."

"Carrie," he murmured.

"You know her?"

"You could say that."

Cole took off for his truck at a dead run. Spinning tires and spraying gravel as he gunned it out of the parking lot, he drew the attention of the nearby spectators who all stopped to watch when several cop cars and one black Ford hit the pavement.

His heart dropped into his stomach when he whipped into her parking lot and saw several more police cars parked. Five cops, each crouched behind their doors with their guns drawn and pointed at the front door of the store, met his gaze. Cole jumped out of his truck and hurried behind one of the cop cars.

"What's going on?" The policeman turned and shot him a questioning look like he wanted to ask what the hell difference it made to him. "I'm a friend of Carrie's."

The cop shook his head before he answered. "Robbery in progress. We aren't sure how many perps or what's going on yet."

"Are Carrie and Jessica in there?"

"Don't know for sure, but it appears so. You can see shadows moving around."

As the words left the policeman's lips, Cole saw the door of the store open. The light from inside reflected behind the two people when they moved outside, making it difficult to discern who they were.

"Everyone back off, or the little lady here takes a bullet," the burglar shouted.

A shadow of what appeared to be two people moved closer to them, and when they did, Cole could see a man with a ski mask over his face holding Carrie in front of him. Cole shifted, ready to move so he could get her away from the crazy guy, until the cop next to him stopped him with a hand on his arm.

"That'll just get you killed, mister. Let us handle this."

"But he's got Carrie."

"I know, but we have to do this the right way so she doesn't get hurt." The policeman shot him a sympathetic look. "I care about her, too. I've known her since she was little, and I hung out with her dad, but rushing the guy will just get her shot."

Cole settled back down next to the cop behind the door of the car. "So what do we do?"

"We negotiate."

"What? We don't have time to negotiate!"

"Calm down. The sheriff over there behind the car to your left will handle this."

Cole grumbled under his breath and the cop chuckled. "By the way, what's your name?"

"Cole Wilder."

"Nice to meet you, Cole. I'm Adam Robinson. I went to high school with Carrie's dad."

Cole gave Adam an exasperated look. Why were they just sitting there doing nothing? Someone needed to do something!

"Known Carrie long?"

"No." His gaze shifted back to the scene in front of him. Cole was fully aware of the amused sparkle in Adam's eyes.

"Kind of gets to you, doesn't she?"

"Yeah. She sure does."

The Captain barked over the megaphone. "Let her go. You can't get away, you know. We've got you surrounded."

"Not a chance, pig. I'm leaving, and she's getting me out of here."

Cole watched as the burglar shifted along toward where her truck was parked, pulling her with him. He couldn't just sit there and do nothing. He needed to help her, somehow.

"Hey!" Adam said, but Cole ignored him and shifted toward the back of the car.

Crouched where he was, he didn't think the man holding Carrie saw him, so Cole worked his way from one police car to another, getting closer and closer to Carrie's truck.

When he had himself positioned on the driver's side, he peeked over the bed to see the burglar almost directly in front of the vehicle. His heart hammering in his chest, he slowly opened the driver's side door that Carrie left unlocked. The police had the man talking, keeping him occupied enough he didn't notice what Cole did until he and the robber were mere feet apart.

"Mister."

The criminal spun around, continuing to hold Carrie by the throat. Her terrified eyes met his as he saw her mouth his name.

"Who the hell are you?"

"Just let her go. You can take me instead."

"Get the hell away from the truck. I'm taking her. She's worth more than you anyway, cowboy."

Cole shrugged like he didn't care. "That may be true." He could see out of the corner of his eye that the police were moving closer while he kept the man talking. "Hey—you ever heard of the Wilders out of Wyoming?" The burglar obviously searched his mind if Cole read his narrowed eyes correctly.

"Maybe."

"I'm the youngest son. If you let her go, you can ransom me. My family would pay dearly to get me back."

The man seemed to contemplate the latest development while he loosened his hold on Carrie's neck slightly. Cole could see the plan when it hatched in her mind, and he tried to communicate to her not to do anything stupid.

Before he had a chance to react, Carrie dropped her hand from the guy's arm, bent her arm at the elbow and jammed it into his gut. The air whooshed from his lungs when he let go of her throat. The guy's eyes opened wide, and he dropped to his knees with a painful groan when her fist connected with his balls. The gun flew out of his hand and skidded across the pavement in Cole's direction.

He almost laughed when she turned around and kicked the guy in the face, knocking him out cold. She stood over the unconscious man as she yelled, "That's for hitting me!"

The fight drained out of her when she turned around and almost flew across the distance separating them, straight into his arms. Stroking her back, he pulled her tight as he whispered in her ear. She clung to him, and her shoulders shook with sobs. The wetness on his shirt broke his heart. A moment later, he was stunned when another set of female arms wrapped around them both.

Jessica ran her hands down Carrie's back and whispered, "Are you okay? God, Carrie! I thought he was going to kill you!"

Cole wrapped both women in his embrace as they reassured each other that they were all right. "Come on. I'm taking you two home," he said while he shuffled them toward his truck. He opened the door, and they slid inside, but before he could shut the door, Carrie stopped him.

"What about the store?"

"I'll talk to the police. They'll have to investigate, anyway. I'm sure they'll lock up when they are done. I'll be right back."

Finding the Captain, Cole stopped next to him and waited.

"Something I can do for you?" The officer looked suspiciously at him. *A thank you would be nice.* He didn't need to make any enemies in this town.

"I just wanted to let you know I'm taking Carrie and Jessica home."

"I'll need their statements before they leave."

"I'm sure you do. Can't it wait until later?"

"No, mister, it can't. I also need to talk to you and find out what your involvement is in this."

Cole stuck out his hand and said, "Cole Wilder. I'm a friend of Carrie's."

The sheriff took his hand and shook it firmly. "Sherriff Williams. I appreciate you wanting to help Carrie, but what you did was stupid, careless, and could have gotten her or one of my officers killed."

"Sorry, Sheriff. I'm kind of impatient that way."

Sheriff Williams' eyes narrowed, and he fixed Cole with a penetrating stare. "You plan on staying in my town, son?"

Cole's shoulder lifted in a shrug. "I'm only here for the rodeo."

"I'd appreciate it if you'd move on soon afterwards. I don't need your kind of trouble in my town."

Well, so much for not making enemies.

"One of the officers will be over there to get their statement in a minute and yours, too. Then, and only then, will you be free to leave."

"Yes, sir," Cole said through clenched teeth before returned to his truck.

"What did they say?"

"They need a statement from all of us before you can leave."

She laid her hand on his arm. "It's okay. We'll be fine."

He ran his fingers through his hair. "I only wanted to get you away from this."

"I know, Cole." Her lips pressed against his cheek for a second before she leaned back and gave him a small smile. "Let's get this over with."

Adam and one other officer approached his truck, separated him from Carrie and Jessica, and took their statements.

"What you did was pretty stupid, Cole," Adam said while he wrote out Cole's statement on his notepad.

"I'm aware of the feelings of the Sheriff, Adam. He's already told me to leave town when the rodeo is over."

"Sorry, son, but we don't need heroics. I know you were worried about Carrie and all."

Carrie and Jessica approached from behind Cole and Carrie said, "Hey, Adam. I didn't realize you were out here, too." She reached up and kissed Adam on the cheek.

"Hey, baby girl. Hey, Jess. You two all right?" Adam wrapped an arm around her shoulder. "Yeah, you know me. I'm always in the thick of things."

A warm chuckle left her lips, and she moved to Cole's side and slipped her arm around his waist. "Yeah, just shook up. Cole is going to take me and Jess home. Can you make sure everything is locked up when the investigation is over?"

"Sure, honey." The officer frowned. "Any idea who this guy was?"

"No. I've never seen him before. My guess is he's not from around here. You know this town, everyone knows everyone."

"Probably not from here then." Adam looked back toward the front of the store. "You go on home. I'll lock up."

"Thanks, Adam."

"No problem. I'll check on you two tomorrow."

Carrie and Jessica waved before Cole ushered them into the cab of his truck and started it.

The trip back to their house was a quiet one. The terror he felt when he heard about the robbery over the radio bothered him. He didn't think twice about skipping his turn to find out what was going on at Carrie's store.

I'm getting in way over my head. Caring about her is getting me nowhere and nowhere fast.

The headlights of his truck spread out into the darkness as they pulled into the yard in front of the house. He didn't open his door until Carrie asked, "Aren't you coming in?"

"Uh…yeah." He couldn't have said no if he tried. He wanted to be near her, wanted to make sure she was all right after her ordeal, but most of all, he didn't want to leave.

Once they were inside, Carrie flipped on the lights, and Jessica moved off toward the stairs. "I'm going up to my room and leave you two alone."

"You don't have to do that, Jess."

She shook her head and smiled but didn't say another word before she walked up the stairs.

They stood in the middle of the room eyeing each other. He was afraid to touch her—afraid he wouldn't be able to be near her without stripping off her clothes in a rush and burying himself in her sweet warmth. He balled his hands into fists inside his pockets to keep from reaching out to her.

* * * *

She dropped her gaze and smiled. He looked so nervous standing by the couch—like he was afraid to come close. Lifting her head, their gazes met for a moment before she walked to him and slipped her arms around his waist, laying her head on his shoulder.

"Just hold me," she whispered, burying her nose in the crook of his neck, inhaling his intoxicating scent. She sighed when she felt his arms wrap around her. It felt so good to have him hold her.

She was surprised when she saw him stand up and try negotiating with the crazy man who held her captive. He had been willing to trade his own safety for hers. What kind of man would do that? They hadn't even known each other more than a few days, but he'd been willing to let the guy take him hostage if he let her go.

When she lifted her head, he growled low in his throat. He lifted his hand, wrapped it in her hair before his mouth dove for hers. Fitting his lips against hers, his tongue speared inside her mouth to capture her moan when she released it. The kiss wasn't the soft, coaxing, playful kisses they'd shared before. This was an all-consuming, full-blown need that raced along her nerves, settling somewhere between them.

His mouth left hers to nibble her lips before moving across her cheek and then down her neck. She tipped her head back and gave him unobstructed access to the hollows of her throat. She arched against him when his palm slipped over her nipple and it hardened beneath his touch.

He lifted his head, framing her face with his hands. "I should have killed him myself for hurting you," he whispered when his thumb moved over the large bruise that had begun to show on her cheek. Dipping his head, he kissed her softly along the bruise.

"Fuck me, Cole. Help me forget the ugliness of what happened tonight."

His eyes searched her face for a moment before he swept her up in his arms and headed for the stairs and her room. Once they were inside, he kicked the door closed with his foot. Laying her softly across the comforter, his hand went to the front of his shirt, but she stopped him and reached for the buttons. She didn't want soft—she didn't want slow, she wanted him now, buried inside her as she screamed his name. Grabbing his shirt in the middle of his chest, she fisted the two halves in her hands and pulled. Surprise registered on his face when the buttons flew in several directions. She tugged the shirt off his shoulders, pinning his arms at his sides before she smiled and rocked back, bringing him down beside her on the bed. Straddling his hips, she sucked his nipple, bringing a groan to his lips.

"Carrie." he growled through clenched teeth as he fought for control.

"Mmm." She didn't lift her mouth while she licked his chest. When she finally released his arms, he reached for her shirt and lifted it over her head. He unhooked her bra and pulled it off too. He reached for the waistband of her jeans, but she shimmied down his body, licking and nibbling his skin.

He wrapped his fingers in her hair when she worked her way toward his cock straining against his pants. Reaching his waist, she slipped the button loose, and he lifted his hips before she stripped them down around his thighs, freeing him to her lips. A groan rumbled in his chest when she ran her tongue across the tip of his cock, the salty taste of his pre-cum sending her own passion out of control. Wrapping her hand around him, she let her palm caress his entire length, and he hissed. She licked her lips before she took him in her mouth, sucking him deep inside. His hips jerked toward her, and she felt his hands tighten in her hair, her name slipping from between his lips. She took his full length into her mouth until his cock bumped the back of her throat.

"God, Carrie. Stop," he growled.

He tugged her up and rolled them over so she was beneath him. His hand found her nipple, rolling it between this thumb and finger until electricity shot straight to her pussy. He let his hand slip down between them, whispering softly against her skin.

"I need you," she whimpered when he undid her jeans and pulled them off. He slipped his hand through the curls and tongued the nipple beneath his mouth. She moaned low in her throat and grasped the back of his head. His fingers spread her apart, and his thumb rubbed against her clit. Warm liquid spilled from her pussy while she continued to groan and wiggle her hips. One of his fingers dove inside, and she almost screamed at the sensation. "Please…"

He finger fucked her for several moments, and she was just about to demand he get it on when he removed his fingers from inside her and reached for his jeans. A condom appeared between his fingers a moment later.

Her tongue slipped along the surface of her lips when he rolled the slippery latex over his proud shaft. He gave her a small smile before he moved between her thighs. She lifted her buttocks off the bed when the tip of his cock rubbed against her clit. Her eyes closed when he slipped inside and filled her.

"God, you feel like heaven," he whispered against her lips, his hips riding hers in a slow, rhythmic dance meant to bring her to the brink.

She whimpered and lifted her buttocks higher, wanting him deeper. He brought her calves up on his arms and tilted his hips, pushing as far as he could. After several strokes, he let her legs down and grabbed her hips while he pounded into her.

Opening her eyes, she could see his blue gaze sparkling in the moonlight filtering through the window. "Come with me. I want to feel you grip me tight, milking everything I have."

She moaned, and the walls of her vagina started to contract. She could feel the pressure building inside her, waiting to burst behind her eyelids and coat her with warmth.

Cole murmured above her, "Oh, God." His hips surged against her as his name spilled from her mouth on a scream.

Chapter Eight

The moonlight streamed through the gauzy curtains, casting shadows on the walls and across the rug on the floor. The moon was so bright it almost lit the entire room, illuminating their entwined limbs on the bed. His fingers caressed her arm where it lay across his stomach, and she slept peacefully on his chest. He couldn't sleep. Tomorrow loomed in the cloudless sky like a shroud over his head.

He wished he had someone to talk to, but Chase and Abby were still on their honeymoon, and Justin would never understand. His conversation with Abby swept across his mind, and he smiled. She would just say I told you so if he told her about Carrie. He loved Abby like a sister. It made him feel good to know Chase had found someone to love, and Abby was the perfect complement to his brother.

Carrie shifted in her sleep, rubbing her cheek against him before she settled back down and her breathing became even again.

What the hell am I going to do now? Walking away seemed so easy before. Why does it have to be so difficult this time?

He frowned as the confusing thoughts swirled around in his head.

You never cared this much before, his heart murmured, and the frown deepened. He lay there for a long time wishing tomorrow would never come but knowing it inevitably would. He had to leave in the morning, and he would probably never see her again.

The room began to lighten when the sun rose over the horizon, and their time together slowly came to an end. He felt Carrie's lips start to drift over his chest, and he groaned softly. The hand resting on her back the entire night moved up and slipped into her hair. Her mouth found his nipple with the rough pad of her tongue, flicking and nipping until he couldn't stand it anymore.

He flipped her over, bringing her hands up to rest above her head and holding them in place. A teasing smile lifted the corners of her mouth when their eyes met.

"Witch," he whispered before his mouth drifted down and found her ripe nipple with his tongue.

She moaned and arched against him when he lapped at her breast.

You really shouldn't be doing this. It's not fair to her if you make love to her and then walk away, his heart whispered, but he chose to ignore it as his body took over.

"Oh, God, Cole—please."

He let go of her hands and moved down her body with swipes of his tongue, stopping at her belly button to swirl and tease. He kissed her stomach and the inside of her thighs before settling his mouth on her wet pussy. His fingers spread her labia before he sucked on her clit, and her body shuddered at the sensations zipping through her. He alternated between licking and sucking as his fingers slid into her hot warmth. Within moments her vagina started to contract around his fingers, but he pulled back and she let out a tortured groan.

"I want inside you when you come." He slid back up her body, taking her mouth with his while he slipped between her swollen pussy lips. Letting out his own painful growl when he felt her warmth surround him, he whispered, "God, you feel so good. I can't get enough of you."

She wiggled her hips and he thought for sure he would come unglued when she whimpered against his mouth, "Make me come."

His hips rocked against her, and she wrapped her legs around his back and held on. His mouth found her breast, suckling, and licking, until the nipple stood up hard and proud. When he finally felt her start to contract around him, he lifted his chest, bringing her legs up so he could fill her to the hilt. His movements became almost frantic when she moaned his name and his own release rose to the surface. He groaned and slammed against her pelvis with his own as he released his seed deep within her. He felt her squeeze his cock, milking everything he had.

Resting on his elbows lying on both sides of her shoulders, he pressed his forehead to hers, and their breathing slowed. "You okay?"

She smiled wistfully as she looked at him. "Mmm…better than okay."

He groaned when he pulled out of her and rolled onto his back, bringing her along with him so she rested on his chest. He brushed his fingers along her shoulder and behind her neck, letting the strands of her hair slide through them.

The silence stretched between them for some time. He didn't know what to say. Goodbye seemed wrong after what they shared.

The alarm clock on the bedside table beeped before it started playing a country song, and Carrie moved to shut it off. He watched her sit up on the side of the bed and reach for a bathrobe hanging on the wall. She slipped it on, pulling her hair out of the back before she tightened the belt around her waist. When she turned around to face him, he couldn't read her eyes and he frowned.

"I need to get ready to go. The store has to open in about an hour." He didn't reply while he tried to figure out what she thought before she dropped her gaze and moved toward the bathroom.

She went inside and shut the door.

* * * *

She sighed and tipped her head back on her shoulders. Gripping the sink in front of her, she fought the tears that threatened to fall down her cheeks.

What the hell was I thinking? It doesn't matter. He'll leave today, and I'll be right here in Silver Ridge, taking care of the store and Jess until I'm so old no one will want me anyway.

"Carrie, are you all right?"

"Yeah, Cole. I'm fine. I just need to get ready to go. There's coffee downstairs if you want some."

"Okay."

She heard his footsteps retreat out the door of her room and down the stairs. Sighing heavily, she turned on the water, washed her face, put on her makeup and pulled her hair back. Stepping back into her room, her gaze stopped on the bed with its tangled sheets and the scent of sex in the air. She shook her head.

It won't do any good to linger on what happened. It's done, over, and he's leaving.

Grabbing some clean clothes, she slipped on her jeans and blouse before heading downstairs for a light breakfast and coffee. "What are you doing?" She laughed when she spotted Cole. He didn't seem the type to cook and here he was, scrambling eggs on the stove.

"Cooking. What's it look like?" He smiled as their eyes met, flashing those devastating dimples in her direction, making her heart skip a beat. "Coffee is on the table. This will be ready in a minute."

"You are making me breakfast?" She cocked an eyebrow, and her lips lifted at the corners. When she took a seat at the dining room table, she was surprised to find the coffee doctored exactly the way she liked it.

"Sure. I figured you could probably use some before you go to the store."

He dished up the eggs and put some toast on the plate along with a couple of pieces of bacon before he sat it down in front of her. Bending down, he stole a quick kiss before he took the other seat across from her.

A piece of meat crunched between her teeth while she studied him. He confused her with his behavior and attentiveness. Wasn't he supposed to just get dressed and leave? Not that she normally had short-term relationships, but that's what she always heard anyway. He sure didn't seem to be in any hurry to go.

"Where is the next rodeo?"

He flashed a grin before he answered. "Are you trying to get rid of me?"

"N–no," she stammered and dropped her gaze to her plate.

He put a finger under her chin, forcing to her to look at him. "I'm kidding, Carrie. Jimmy and I are headed to Crawford, Nebraska. There is a rodeo this coming weekend."

"Oh." *Damn it! Jimmy needs to own up to his responsibility, but I shouldn't get Cole involved. It's not fair to him. He is Jimmy's friend, though.*

Cole cocked his head to the side and stared. "What's wrong, Carrie?"

"You're Jimmy's friend, but…"

"Yeah."

"Jess hasn't told me if she's talked with him about the baby, but tell him he needs to do right by her. Otherwise, she'll get a paternity test when it's born, and he'll be forced to at least pay child support."

"I'll tell him."

"Where are you going after Crawford?" Catching her lip between her teeth, she chewed it for a moment. She wanted to feel nonchalant about Cole's leaving, but something tugged at her insides, something she didn't want to think about it.

His fingers raked through his hair, and her hand itched to comb an errant curl back in place. "Does it matter?"

"Never mind. It's none of my business."

The rest of their breakfast was eaten in silence even if she could feel every time his gaze rested on her face. When they were both done, she grabbed the plates and slid them inside the sink.

A moment later, he pressed against her back and his lips brushed her neck. Shivers rolled down her spine and she tipped her head, desperately wanting his mouth on her skin.

Good Lord, I'm pathetic for wanting him like this.

"I wish we had time."

"Time?"

"I've never wanted anyone like I want you, Carrie. I can't seem to get enough."

"Oops. Sorry."

Jessica stood in the doorway when Carrie turned. "It's okay, Jess. Cole was just leaving."

A frown swept across his face before he said, "Uh…yeah."

"I'll walk you out." Tears threatened to choke her, but she refused to let him see how much his leaving hurt. With a smile plastered on her face, she grabbed his hat from where he left it on the couch the night before and handed it to him.

"Thanks." He looked like he wanted to say something else when he shot her a confused glance. After a moment, he shook his head and grabbed the handle on the front door. Once outside, she realized her truck was still at the store.

"Looks like I'll have to take you to work."

"Yeah, I guess so. I seemed to keep forgetting where my vehicle is when you are around." A frustrated sigh spilled from between her lips. "Let me grab my keys and I'll be back in a second."

She retreated inside and when she caught Jessica's amused expression, she frowned.

"Forget something?"

"Yeah. My truck is still at the store."

"He tends to do that to you, doesn't he?"

"Shut up, Jess," she said when she reached for her purse and keys with her sister's laughter ringing in her ears. "I'll see you at the store at eleven."

Not waiting for an answer, she went out the front door, slamming it behind her and grumbling under her breath about annoying sisters. Cole stood leaning against his truck, arms crossed over his broad chest with a Cheshire cat grin.

Damn, why does he have to be so gorgeous!

The store was only a few minutes from the house. Within a short time, they were pulling into the parking lot.

She got out on the passenger side without waiting for him and walked toward the door. He followed her inside, and they moved toward the office only to find a huge mess. There were papers strewn everywhere. The office door stood open, and it looked like a bomb had gone off in there. The case where the silver jewelry and belt buckles were kept lay broken in several pieces from what she decided had probably been a stray bullet when the man shot the register.

"What a fucking mess!"

"I'll help you clean it up." Cole started picking up paperwork off the floor, stacking it neatly and placing it on the desk.

"I thought you were leaving for Nebraska this morning?"

"We are, but I have a little time."

She looked around and shook her head. "I can't open the store like this. I'll have to stay closed today so I can clean up."

"How about you make some kind of a sign to put on the door, and I'll work on cleaning up this glass? I'm sure your customers will understand. The whole town probably knows about the robbery."

"You're probably right. Silver Ridge isn't that big of a place."

Cole reached for a broom and dustpan as she grabbed some paper to make a small sign for the door. Working in compatible silence, they got most of the glass cleaned up and the items in the case moved into the office so they could be locked up.

They spent the morning attempting to right everything in the store.

The cell phone on his hip started to ring. Unclipping it, he stared at the screen a moment before his gaze shot to hers across the room. He flipped it open and said, "Yeah."

The voice on the other end came across in a murmur, but she gathered from the conversation the caller was Jimmy and he wanted to know when they were leaving.

"In a little bit. It's not that far to Crawford." His eyes met hers and she tried not to let him see the hurt she felt when she thought of him leaving.

How stupid! I've known all along he would leave when the rodeo ended. I shouldn't be torn up about this.

"All right." He hung up the phone with a click. A soft knock on the window tore her gaze from his. Without a word, she went to the door and unlocked it for her sister. Once Jessica was inside, she relocked and met her sister's gaze.

"You stayed closed?"

"Yeah. There was too much of a mess in here to let customers in today."

Jessica's gaze took in Cole's presence before her attention returned to her sister. They moved in tandem toward him.

"Hey, Cole."

"Jess."

"I thought you and Jimmy were leaving this morning."

"We are."

"Tell him to expect to hear from an attorney since he doesn't want to admit this child is his."

Cole's eyebrows rose. "Uh…I'll make sure he knows. I need to get going. Walk out with me." It wasn't a request. It was a command and one Carrie willingly followed, wanting to keep him with her just a little bit longer.

He wrapped his arm around her shoulder, and they walked out together through the side door. Tears burned her eyelids, and her heart felt like it was shattering when they approached his truck.

I'm not going to cry. I'm not going to let him know how much this hurts. It was supposed to be a no-strings-attached weekend and that's exactly what he's going to think it was.

He unlocked the truck before he stopped next to the door and wrapped his arms around her. She inhaled his unique scent, all male and oh-so-sexy, when she buried her nose in his neck. She wanted to remember this, remember him, how it felt for him to hold her so she could pretend he loved her as much as she loved him.

Love him? No—I won't do that. I can't fall in love with him. A sob caught in her throat and she forced it down with a swallow. *I won't cry. I won't cry.*

He pushed her back and looked down into her eyes, and she almost lost it, almost let him know how she felt.

"It was fun while it lasted, huh?"

God, that hurt.

"Yeah. You know, next time you're in Silver Ridge, look me up."

"Sure. Never know when I might find myself somewhere close by. There are always rodeos all over these parts."

She stepped back and shrugged, wrapping her arms around her waist as she tried to hold her heart together. "Thanks for all your help the last few days."

"I'm glad I was there for you." Brushing his fingers down her cheek for a second, he slid his hand toward her ear and tucked a stray strand of hair behind it. His hand went behind her head before his lips slanted across hers. All the desperation and need flowed from her lips when his mouth took hers and his tongue slid between her lips to caress hers.

When he finally released her and stepped back, his gaze held hers for a moment. "Bye, Carrie."

She couldn't watch—didn't want to see him pull out of her parking lot and never to return. The sound of his truck pulling out onto the highway ripped her heart in half. Jessica wrapped her in a warm hug. A moment later, wracking sobs shook her frame and the tears rolled down her cheeks.

Chapter Nine

The snow whipped across the flat fields, blurring everything except what was within a few feet. Winter in Wyoming hit hard every year, but this one seemed especially bleak. Cole stood at the door of the barn and pulled the collar of his coat up around his ears before he started toward the house.

"Damn, it's cold." A shiver rolled down his back as he stomped his feet to loosen the snow from his boots. Abby would kill him if he tracked snow in the house. He smiled when he thought of his sister-in-law. She sure was grumpy these days, but being pregnant did that to a gal he guessed. Having not spent a lot of time around a pregnant woman, he wasn't quite sure.

Leaning his shoulder against the wooden door, he pushed it open and then slammed it shut again while the howling wind whipped outside. Hanging his coat on the rack, he toed off his boots, leaving them near the door.

"Hey. Would you like some coffee?" Abby asked.

"You bet. It can't be more than about five degrees out there with that wind."

"Well, nobody said you had to work the mare today. And that Mack truck of Mike Carroll's could have waited a day or two for your talented hands." Abby gave him a playful smirk from the kitchen. "I know you want to keep busy, though. It must suck to have this down time from all the rough rodeo stuff."

"Yeah. I need to keep my mind busy."

She cocked an eyebrow in his direction, but he wasn't talking. He hadn't said anything to Chase or Abby about Carrie, but he had a gut feeling she already knew. After all, she told him way back when he would meet his match, and he was afraid she was right. He hadn't been able to forget about the hazel-eyed beauty.

The rest of the summer, he and Jimmy had done the normal thing, going from town to town, winning and losing, but never staying long. He even tried hooking up with some of the women who showed interest, but he couldn't get past the first kiss. Comparing each and every kiss to the rush he felt with Carrie's drove him insane.

"Stop giving me that look, Abby."

She just laughed, and he frowned.

"Are you finally going to give up and tell me about her? You have been back here for several months now. Always keeping silent even though I'm sure being away from her is tearing you up inside."

His head snapped up as he caught her inquisitive look. He lifted his shoulders in a nonchalant shrug.

"Come here and sit with me a minute. I need to get off my feet for a bit." She grabbed his hand and forced him to sit on the couch with her. "Now. About this woman."

"What woman?"

"Don't give me that, Cole Wilder. You obviously need to talk, or would you rather talk to Chase? I'm okay with that if you would rather talk to him, you know, guy to guy. Sometimes it's easier to talk to another man than a woman about matters of the heart."

Air rushed from between his lips in a heavy sigh when he realized he might as well give into her demanding tone. Ever since the day he first laid eyes on Abby, he had never been able to keep a secret from her. Her sensitive nature made her more aware of things around her and the people nearby, but it kind of gave him the creeps.

"All right."

"Good." She grinned and tucked her feet under her and got comfortable. Obviously this was going to be a *long* conversation.

"Jimmy and I went to Silver Ridge, South Dakota back at the beginning of the season. It was one of the first rides, and I didn't want to miss it. It was right after you and Chase got married. In fact, I think you were still on your honeymoon."

She blushed slightly, and he smiled.

"Where is my brother anyway?" He scooted to the edge of the couch as he started to stand. "He could probably use some help and I…"

"Sit your cute little ass back down on that couch and quit trying to change the subject."

"You aren't going to let me get out of telling you this, are you?"

"Nope—continue."

He let his thoughts drift back to the first meeting with Carrie and how she ripped into him in the bar that night. "The first night we were there, we had stopped at a place to get a couple of beers before we bedded down for the night." He pressed his hand against his chest, just about where his heart lay when it ached for the woman he left behind. "A woman came in and started jumping my shit about her sister and how she was pregnant with my kid."

Abby's eyes widened with shock.

"Don't worry. It was a mistake."

"I'm glad. I can't see you getting someone pregnant and walking away from your responsibility."

A crooked smile crossed his face before he frowned. "Thanks, I think."

"You're welcome."

"Anyway, after we figured out everything was a mistake and Jimmy had actually gotten the woman's sister pregnant, she apologized and left."

"That's it?" She eyed him suspiciously. "I know there is more to this than you are telling so fess up."

He shrugged. *Maybe I can get away with not telling her. Then again, maybe not. Abby is too aware of everything around her.*

Abby took his hand in hers and closed her eyes for a moment before a wicked little grin crossed her face. He pulled his hand back. "Stop doing that, would you?"

"Well, if you aren't going to tell me, I have to find out somehow because I know there's something you are holding back." Her lips lifted in a grin.

"All right. All right." He stood up and began pacing in front of the fire. "I won that competition, by the way."

"Congratulations."

"Thanks."

"Now get back to the story and quit stalling."

He rolled his eyes before he continued. "We talked some more and she apologized again. I asked her out after my ride. She went and watched from the stands until I had finished and then we had planned on meeting back by my truck to figure out what we were going to do." He stopped pacing and ran his fingers through his hair.

"And?"

"After my ride, I walked back to my truck and stood there taking off my chaps when I felt a hand on my ass. When I turned around, a blonde wrapped her arms around me and plastered her lips against mine."

"Uh…I'm sure that just broke your heart, having some pretty woman throw herself at you."

He chuckled. "It wouldn't have been, except the other woman saw it and got pissed off."

"Why don't you just call her Carrie so I know who you are talking about?"

His gaze ricocheted to Abby sitting on the couch. *How the hell did she know Carrie's name?* "But I never told you her name."

She just shook her head and smiled.

"That's just creepy, Abby."

"Sorry. I can't help it. Blame my mother. Do you have any idea how hard it was to keep anything from her?"

A soft chuckle left his mouth. "I can imagine."

"Okay. Go on."

He shrugged and continued to pace. "Not much else to tell. She met me at the bar later that night. We were having a good time and some guy got up on the stage and announced to everyone he and Carrie were getting married."

"Okkaayy…" Her eyes searched his face, and he frowned.

"Evidentially he and Carrie had known each other since they were young and he had been asking her to marry him for several years. He was really drunk, but when I heard him say that, I got mad and took off. She caught me at my truck and explained. And…" He wasn't sure how much detail he wanted to go into with Abby. If she already knew Carrie's name, she could probably sense how intimate the two of them had been. He sat back down on the couch as sympathy swept across Abby's face.

"Are you going to see her again?"

"I don't know." He wanted to. God knew he wanted to, but he wasn't sure how to go about things. Two days after he left her side, when he had gotten into Crawford, he realized he didn't even have her phone number. Oh, he knew the name of the store, of course, and could probably call directory assistance to at least get that number, but he just wasn't sure how receptive she would be to his phone call. *It was just a weekend fling, wasn't it?* Normally, women came easy to him with his blonde, blue-eyed looks and dimpled smile, and he rarely had a woman turn him down.

"Have you even talked to her since you left?"

"No."

"Cole Wilder! I can't believe you!"

"What?"

"You haven't even called her?"

He dipped his head sheepishly. Abby's indignant tone made him feel like shit. "No."

Abby grumbled. "It would be a wonder if she would even talk to you now. Six months—six months and you haven't even called her." She struggled up from her place on the couch and grabbed the phone as she continued to grumble. "Jeesus…sleep with her then don't call her for six friggin' months. Men!"

"What are you doing?" *I don't like the looks of this.*

"I'm going to call her for you, and you are going to talk to her."

He pulled the phone from her grasp. "No, you aren't. I can't talk to her, not right now."

"Well, then I suggest you get your butt in that truck of yours and go see her." Her hands on her hips, she tapped her foot impatiently. He almost laughed at the picture she presented.

"She probably won't even talk to me."

"Then you aren't any worse off than you are right now. You are miserable thinking about her and wondering, so take the leap, Cole, and find out if what you feel is the real thing."

"I don't know what I feel, Abby." He raked his fingers through his hair again.

"You care about her, don't you?"

He shrugged, trying to be nonchalant. He couldn't fool Abby, so he wasn't sure why he even tried. "Yeah. I guess so. I mean, I wonder how the store is doing and how she's handling things on her own. She's so independent. She reminds me a lot of you. I get the feeling she can do just fine without a man in her life."

"Just because she might be able to handle things doesn't mean she necessarily wants to. Maybe she wants a guy to take care of her for a change instead of her having to shoulder all the responsibility? Did you ever think of that?"

Abby's words made sense. It was driving him crazy not knowing. "It would take me a few days to get there with the snow."

"Then I suggest you get moving before it snows more. You know better than I how the storms roll through Wyoming in the winter."

He chuckled dryly. Born and raised in Laramie, he knew all too well how finicky the weather could be. He finally let himself believe going to see Carrie would be a good thing.

Maybe then I can at least put some things to rest.

Reaching over and pulling Abby into a warm hug, he said, "Thanks, sis. You always know exactly what to say."

She playfully punched him in the shoulder. "Only with stubborn men by the last name of Wilder and maybe one still single female Wilder."

"What are you going to do when this baby comes? If it's a boy, he'll probably be just like his dad, but if it's a girl…"

"He'll be just as stubborn as his father and his uncles."

"He?" She smiled secretively and dropped her gaze a moment before he forced her gaze back to his. "Does Chase know?"

"I don't even know."

"You don't lie very well, Abby."

"Just a feeling, Cole."

"And we all know how your *feelings* are." He kissed her on the cheek. "Congratulations. I can't wait to hear what Chase says."

"Don't you dare tell him."

"I won't, but you know he's going to be mad I know before he does."

"Going to be mad you know what, little brother?" Neither Cole nor Abby heard the back door when Chase came into the house, but obviously he overheard some of their conversation.

"Nothing, bro. I've got an errand to run. I won't be home for a while, I'm thinkin'."

"Oh? Going somewhere?" Chase moved to Abby's side and tucked her under his arm. She snuggled into his warmth.

"Yeah—to see a woman."

Shock was written all over Chase's face, and he almost laughed. "A woman?" Chase looked at Abby and then to him. "I didn't just hear you say you are going to see a woman, did I? Not permanent bachelor Cole Wilder."

"Yes and don't you start. I've already had this conversation with your wife." Cole shot Abby a playful wink.

"Well then, I'll just have to get it from her," Chase growled playfully as he pulled Abby in front of him and nuzzled her neck. Abby laughed as she tried to wiggle from her husband's grasp.

Cole chuckled, heading for his room to pack some things to take with him as Chase swept Abby in his arms and moved in the opposite direction. He shook his head, his own thoughts sobering.

What will Carrie say when she sees me again? Would she throw herself in my arms or give me the cold shoulder?

He didn't know but he was about to find out, and the thought had him worried.

* * * *

"Damn, Carrie. Can't we turn on the heat in here? It's cold."

Carrie stood by the wood stove in the corner of the store, warming her hands with the heat. The store was frigid, but this time of year they had to conserve money. Winter hit hard in the north, and it was no different in Silver Ridge, South Dakota. The snow continued to fall in beautiful, glistening crystal flakes as the tinkling of Christmas music could be heard over the radio.

"Sorry, Jess, we can't. Come over here and sit by the wood stove where it's warmer."

Jessica struggled to her feet, cradling her large abdomen with her hands as she moved to the rocking chair sitting nearby. Groaning, she lowered herself into the chair before she sighed.

"Are you feeling okay?"

"Yeah—other than grumpy and wanting this baby to finally get here, I'm fine."

Carrie laughed. "You still have a month to go."

"I know and I don't know how I will survive. My feet are swollen, my back hurts, and I just want this over with. This baby is going to weigh a ton before he finally makes his appearance."

"I tell you what, after we close in an hour, I'll rub your back for you."

"Would you? That would be heavenly."

"Of course I will. I know you are uncomfortable."

"Can't we just close now? I mean, we've hardly had a customer all day."

"No, we can't. The sign says we are open until five and that's what time we'll close."

"I know, but only an idiot would be out in this snow."

The bell over the door tinkled. "Well, obviously there is an idiot out today. I'll go see what it is. You stay here and keep warm."

"You won't hear an argument out of me. Let me know if you need help, though."

"I will."

Carrie headed for the front of the store. Jessica's observation was correct. There weren't many people out today, and only those desperate for feed for their livestock or those that hadn't already stocked their supplies were adventurous enough to be out in this weather.

She moved behind the counter but couldn't see who came in except a black Stetson over the shelving down one aisle. The hat made her heart clench before she beat it down with a stern talking to.

Forget him. He obviously didn't care enough to even keep in contact. It was almost six months to the day when he left Silver Ridge with a kiss and a quick goodbye.

Shaking her head to clear her thoughts, she moved in the direction of the customer.

Turning the corner of the aisle she started to say, "Can I help…"

He turned around, and her heart skipped a beat when his blue eyes crinkled at the corners as his lips lifted in a smile.

"Cole?" She took two steps forward before she stopped. "Oh my God, Cole," she whispered before her feet flew across the few feet separating them and launching herself into his arms.

Chapter Ten

He wrapped his arms around the beautiful woman who had thrown herself in his arms while his heart sighed.

God, it feels good to hold her.

It had been a hellacious twelve-hour trip from Laramie to Silver Ridge. He had almost put himself in the ditch on several occasions, but he finally made it to her house only to find it empty. Getting back in his truck, he made the short trek to the store, not at all surprised to find the store open.

She pushed against his shoulders, and he released her a little, but he wasn't going to let her go anytime soon. He wanted to feel her lips under his so badly he ached with need. His eyes met hers and, with a tortured growl, he swooped down and took her mouth with his. She wrapped her hands in the hair at the nape of his neck as she moaned softly. Letting himself deepen the kiss when she opened for him, his tongue swept inside her mouth, dueling with hers while heat spread through him. His hand found the underside of her breast, sliding along her nipple, exciting him further when he felt it harden to his touch. She groaned into his mouth and pushed her breast further into his palm.

God, I want her.

He was stunned at how much he missed her and how good she felt in his arms.

"Carrie?"

Jessica's panicked voice brought him out of his passion-filled fog. He pulled his mouth from Carrie's, and they stepped apart.

"Carrie!"

Without a word, she whipped around and raced for the back of the store. He was hot on her heels as all kinds of thoughts raced through his mind.

He reached the back where Jessica's high-pitched voice rattled off incoherent while Carrie tried to calm her. "It's okay, Jess. Calm down. Everything will be fine."

Not quite sure what was going on, his worried expression met Carrie's across the room. He took in Jessica's large abdomen, stunned that for moment he'd forgotten about her having Jimmy's child. His mind had been so wrapped up in seeing Carrie again and having her in his arms her sister hadn't even crossed his mind.

"What's wrong?"

"She needs to get to the hospital. I think her water broke."

His gaze swept down Jessica's body only to find the large wet spot on the floor at her feet. "What do we do?"

"How were the roads?"

"Slick."

"Shit." Carrie cursed, but he could see her mind working, trying to think of some way to get her sister where she needed to be. "Can you drive us to the hospital?"

"Of course, but it'll be slow going."

"We've got to do something, otherwise she'll be having this baby right here in the store." Carrie walked quickly to the pile of blankets on the shelf, grabbing several before she moved back to her sister's side. "Wrap these around you. I'm going to lock up really fast." Her eyes turned back to him. "Can you take her out to your truck? Yours is four-wheel drive, right? Mine isn't running the best, and I don't want to chance breaking down."

"Yeah, but do you think this is such a good idea? I mean, what if we get stuck somewhere and she has the baby in my truck?"

"We have to do something, Cole. We can't stay here." Her terse tone grated on his nerves. Concern for Jess warred with his need to take Carrie in his arms and kiss the daylights out of her again while she ordered him around. "Get moving. We need to get her there now."

Grumbling under his breath about stubborn females, he moved toward Jessica and said, "Come on, Jess." He helped her wrap the blanket around her before he steered her in the direction of the front entrance. Carrie came up behind them a moment later and opened the door. The frigid wind whipped around them as he hustled Jessica out to his truck and Carrie pulled the door shut behind them. When all three of them were settled, he slowly pulled out onto the highway.

"Which way?"

Carrie sat in the middle between him and Jess with her arm around her sister's shoulders. She pointed them in the right direction, but when her attention was drawn back to Jessica, he took a moment to study her. She hadn't changed much in the last six months. Still gorgeous, still full of fire and still bossy, he noticed.

Her murmurs of comfort to Jessica kept his mind on the emergent situation at hand while he continued to pick his way along the slippery highway.

There sure aren't many people out.

"Has the weather been bad here?"

"Yeah," she murmured, but didn't take her gaze off her sister. "It's been snowing heavily for several days."

"Wyoming's been bad, too."

"That where you've been?"

"Since the season ended, yeah."

The lights of the hospital came into view, and he almost sighed with relief. He really didn't want to have to witness a baby's delivery in the cab of his truck. Pulling right into the ambulance bay, he said, "I'll go get help. Stay here and stay warm."

Carrie put a hand on his arm. "Thanks for being here."

He let a small smile play on his lips, and his hand covered hers. "Where else would I be?"

A frown pulled down the corners of her mouth, and her lips parted like she wanted to say something, but he didn't wait. Sliding out into the snow, he felt his feet hit pavement under the six-inch deep drift before he shut the door. Rushing inside, he almost slid on the wet floor as he stopped at the reception desk.

"I need some help, fast."

The young woman's appreciative gaze raked him from the top of his blonde head to the tip of his cowboy boots as she popped the gum in her mouth and grinned. "I bet you do, handsome."

"Not me. I have a pregnant woman in my truck who is going to have a baby. Can you get someone, please?" He wasn't in the mood for a flirtatious woman right at the moment.

"Sure, honey." The woman picked up the phone next to her, dialing with her bright red fingernails. "Hey. There is a guy out here with a pregnant woman in his truck. Can one of you grab a wheelchair? Okay. Thanks." She turned her gaze back to him. "They'll be out in a sec."

"Thanks." He walked to the window and watched the snow swirl in the wind before it hit the ground until he heard someone behind him.

"Which way?"

"Under the ambulance bay."

"Is she in labor?"

"How in the hell am I supposed to know?" He was getting agitated.

These people obviously had no clue what was going on, or did they?

Hell. He'd been around pregnant horses and pregnant cows, but a pregnant woman—he didn't want to go there.

Following the orderly out the door, he directed him to where the truck was parked. They struggled through the snow even though they had obviously shoveled the walk recently and put some kind of salt on the pavement.

When they finally reached the passenger side, he could see Carrie and Jessica talking, but he could also tell something wasn't quite right. Jessica's face was contorted with pain as Carrie tried to calm her. They opened the door as both women turned terrified eyes to him.

I don't like the looks of this. "What's wrong?"

"I don't know. We need to get her inside—quickly," Carrie answered her voice crackling with tears.

"Well, ma'am, if you'll just get in this wheelchair…" The orderly from inside tried moving into position, but Cole stopped him as he reached inside the truck, sweeping Jessica up in his arms, heading for the door.

"Show me where. We don't have time for the damned chair." The orderly finally must have decided not to trifle with him as he opened the ambulance door, ushering the trio inside.

Cole moved inside one of the exam rooms and gently laid Jessica down on the bed as Carrie took the other side, wrapping her sister's hand in her warm one.

One of the nurses came into the room and began preparing things to get Jessica's checked in. "My name is Mandy. I'll be taking care of you while you are in the emergency room."

"Where's the doctor?" Patience was not his virtue, and he knew it, but damn these people were driving him crazy and it wasn't even his wife or his baby.

"Sir, I'm sure your wife will be fine. The doctor will be in here in a minute, but I need to get her into the computer system before we can do anything."

"She's not my wife, she's…" *What the hell is she to me? Nothing, really—just Carrie's sister, but that's enough.*

Carrie was worried, he could see the terror in her eyes and that was enough for him.

"Well, anyway, I need to get her processed. If you'd like to step out, I can get this done a bit quicker."

"Fine." Jamming his hands into his pockets, he flashed Carrie a look meant to reassure her before he pulled open the door and slipped out. He started pacing the hall like an expectant father until Carrie came out a moment later. Without a word, she walked into his arms, wrapping hers around his waist and laying her head on his shoulder while he rubbed her back. "Everything will be okay. We're at the best place for her."

"I know," her murmured words sent a tingle down his arms when they whispered against the skin of his neck. "I'm just scared. It's too early. She's not due for a month."

"Come on. Let's sit down over here. This could take a while." He steered her in the direction of several chairs. When they sat down together side-by-side, he took her hand in his, threading their fingers so he held her soft palm against his. He wrapped his arm around her shoulder and tugged her close while his lips brushed her forehead. "She'll be fine."

"God, I hope so," Carrie whispered, terror so clear in her voice his heart ached for her.

* * * *

Several minutes later, the nurse rushed out and hurried around the desk. Carrie stood and moved toward the room where Jessica lay just as the doctor rushed out, too.

"What's wrong? What's wrong with Jess?"

"Are you family?" She didn't like the look on his face.

"Yes. I'm her sister."

The doctor's gaze stopped on Cole's face before coming back to hers.

"She's bleeding. We need to take the baby and quickly. We are calling in the surgical team right now."

"Oh, my God." She almost collapsed—would have if Cole hadn't grabbed her.

"Are you the father?"

"No. I'm just a friend," Cole answered as he held her up.

"He's with me," she answered. "Can I see her?"

"Of course. It will probably be good for you to be there until we take her to surgery. She's upset, and we'll be giving her something to calm her, but she's scared."

The doctor escorted her and Cole back inside the room. When Carrie moved to her sister's side, Jessica opened her sleepy eyes. She brushed the hair off her sister's forehead, trying to smile encouragingly. "Hey."

"Hi."

Jessica's looked at Cole standing behind her with his hand on her shoulder.

"Take care of Carrie okay? If something happens to me, you have to take care of her."

"Nothin' is going to happen, Jess. You'll be fine." His self-assured voice calmed the whole atmosphere in the room. He was right. He had to be right. Nothing would happen to her sister. It couldn't. She wouldn't be able to handle it, if it did. God couldn't be that cruel, could He? She started to shake, and he wrapped his arms around her waist. Leaning against his side, she tried desperately to absorb his heat and his calm.

The surgical team came in the room and prepared her to be moved. She took Jessica's hand in hers and whispered, "I love you, sis."

"I love you, too, Carrie." They started to move her, but Jessica stopped them. "If something happens and the baby makes it, but I don't, take care of him, okay? Love him like I would have."

"Don't say that, Jess. Everything is going to be fine. You are going to be here to raise this baby."

"Promise me, Carrie—please. "You were always the strong one, you know. Always taking care of me, even when I didn't want you to."

She would do anything for Jessica. "Okay. I promise."

Gripping her sister's hand for a moment, she tried to smile encouragingly. The frightened look in Jessica's eyes did nothing to calm her own fears. Cole stood behind her and all three of them held hands for a moment before they began to move her and they had to let go.

"I'll take care of her, Carrie," Martin Jessup said. He arrived shortly after the surgical team, and he would be performing the surgery on Jess. They had known Martin all their lives. He was there when the girl's were little, bandaging up scrapped knees and broken bones, and he had been with them when their parents died. He was their father's best friend, constant companion, and the strength behind them when they broke the news about their parent's death. He was the man who was supposed to deliver all their children, the best OB-GYN in the whole area.

"I know, Martin." Carrie wiped a tear from her cheek. "Keep her safe for me, okay?"

Martin nodded before he disappeared shortly after the stretcher rolled through the double doors.

She turned around and buried her face against Cole's shoulder. Tears rolled down her face and sobs racked her body while he held her tight.

Chapter Eleven

Carrie and Cole sat there for what seemed like hours, waiting. Every once in a while, she would stand up and pace the waiting area, rubbing her arms to calm the chills, but nothing helped—nothing but Cole's touch.

The moment the doctor came through the double doors, her heart dropped into her stomach at the look in his eyes.

No! It couldn't be!

"The baby is fine. A nice healthy boy."

"Jess?" The words left her mouth in a whisper as she felt Cole behind her, hugging her like he'd never let go.

Martin's eyes filled with tears. It was a sight she'd never forget. "I tried, Carrie. God knows I tried."

"Don't…" She shook her head in denial. "Don't say it. I can't do this again, Martin. I just can't!"

Martin held her close while the sobs racked her body, and they both cried the tears of those who lost people they loved way too soon.

Pushing against her shoulders, he looked down into her eyes. "She's still here—for now, Carrie, but there isn't anything else I can do. She's bleeding internally, and I can't stop it. I've already taken out everything I can."

"What happened?"

"The placenta ruptured, tearing away from the uterus. We are lucky the baby survived, but Jessica has systemic bleeding. In other words, she's bleeding from several areas in her body—her blood is too thin."

"Take mine. I'll give her whatever she needs."

"It won't help, Carrie. I can't give her blood as fast as she losing it."

"Can I see her?"

"Of course." He wrapped his arm around her shoulder to lead her away, but she turned and grasped Cole's hand.

"Come with me. I can't do this by myself."

Cole entwined his fingers with hers as they walked down the hall. Sandwiched between the two men, she felt their strength—the strength of a man too wise for his years in the friend of the family, a man who had seen way too much death in his lifetime. Martin still continued to work as a doctor, delivering babies everyday and sharing in the joy of a new family or the sorrow of a lost one.

Cole's strength became her lifeline, too. She didn't know why God brought him back into her life on this very important day. In her mind, she screamed it wasn't fair for God to take Jess away from her when He'd taken her parents not so long ago. Right now she didn't have the strength to question why Cole was back.

She almost couldn't put one foot in front of the other as they walked. *I so tired, tired of losing the people I love, tired of doing this all alone.*

When they approached the door to one of the hospital rooms, she held back.

"I can't do this," she whispered when her gaze met Cole's.

"Yes, you can, Carrie. She needs your strength right now."

"But how can I say goodbye?"

"I don't know, honey. You'll do just fine, though."

They walked in together, the door closing softly behind them.

She moved toward the bed, her sister's pale form lying in the center with so many wires and tubes hooked to her. Carrie didn't know how she could even reach her. Picking up her hand, she whispered softly, "Jess?"

Jessica opened her eyes and smiled. "Hey."

"Hi." Carrie tried to smile. "How are you feeling?"

"Like shit. How's the baby?"

"He's fine. I haven't seen him yet, but Martin says he's doing okay."

"Good," Jessica whispered as her eyes closed tiredly.

The store opened silently, and the nurse brought the baby in wrapped in a pale blue blanket. "I thought you might like to hold him."

Jessica smiled. The nurse laid the baby on her chest, and she wrapped her arms around him. "I love you, baby boy," Jessica said when tears welled up in her eyes and her gaze returned to Carrie. "I want his name to be Robert, Carrie. Robert Allen Marsh."

Carrie choked back a sob. "I'll make sure of it."

"He's so little." Jessica's finger slipped down the sleeping baby's cheek.

"Jess?" She turned back toward Carrie, her gaze sweeping up to take in Cole standing behind her. "Do you know what's happening?"

"Yeah, sis. Martin told me." Tears slid from the corners of her eyes into her hair. "You promised, remember?"

Carrie choked back a sob as she nodded.

"Take care of him. He's going to need you," Jessica whispered.

Her shoulders shook. "I can't do this without you, Jess."

"Yes, you can, Carrie." Her gaze swung to Cole. "You promised, too, Cole. You have to take care of Carrie."

"I'll do my best." She could hear the tears in his voice, too, as he stood behind her, his hand resting on her shoulder.

Jessica's dim gaze returned to hers and a heart-wrenching smile life her mouth for a moment. "Please make sure he knows who I am though. Make sure he knows I love him and I wanted him, no matter what."

"I will. I'll show him pictures every day of you," Carrie murmured, tears rolling down her cheeks while her heart shattered from the pain.

Jessica closed her eyes. "I have to go now, Carrie. Momma and Daddy are waiting for me."

"I love you, Jess." She reached over and hugged her sister close. "Tell Mommy and Daddy I love them, too, and I miss them terribly."

"I will," Jess whispered.

A moment later, the machine over her head beeped, a long mournful sound that tore through Carrie's heart while she sobbed, holding her sister close.

* * * *

Three days later, she stood solemnly at the side of the casket as it sat perched on the table, waiting to be lowered into the gaping hole in the ground. The whole town turned out for the funeral of Jessica Anne Marsh. People milled about, talking in low whispers when they moved to their cars to leave. The service was over and there wasn't anything left except to lower her into the grave sitting next to her parents.

Carrie lovingly ran her hand over the top of the pearl white casket a moment before she lifted her face to the sun overhead, letting it dry the tears on her cheeks. Hearing the soft mews of the infant, she turned around and had to smile. Cole stood holding the baby in his arms, cradling him softly to his chest. He looked like a natural father. One would never know up until two days ago he'd never held a baby before.

"Here, let me take him."

"Good. He's starting to get fussy, and I don't do babies very well."

She gave him a sad smile and took the baby from his arms. "You could have fooled me."

Her face sobered when he wrapped his arm around her and they walked to his truck. Once inside, she put the baby in his car seat before buckling her seatbelt. They drove back to the house in silence.

The house was eerily quiet. Her gaze swept the room as tears pooled and a sob shook her shoulders.

"Here. I'll change him and put him down." Cole took the baby from her arms before he pushed her down on the couch. "I'll be right back."

She sat in the same spot until he returned. Her head dropped onto his shoulder when he took a seat next to her.

"What am I going to do without her? How am I supposed to take care of a baby? I've never even babysat a newborn."

"It'll be okay. You're a natural, Carrie." He stroked her arm with his hand, calming her nerves and her sobs with his presence.

Does he have any idea what his being here means to me?

He had been back in Silver Ridge four days—four days spent helping her deal with Jessica's death and her burial—four days holding her at night, soothing her when the terrible nightmares woke her.

What am I going to do when he leaves? "Are you opening the store tomorrow?"

"I don't have a choice. It's the only way I can pay the bills."

"I'm sorry, honey, but what about the baby?"

"I'll take him with me. I have Mark who works with me. I'll have to increase his hours."

"I know you'll figure out something, Carrie. You're such an organized, responsible person. You don't know how to be any other way."

She snorted when she heard his words. Until now, they hadn't even had a chance to talk about why he came back and what it meant to their relationship.

Or lack thereof.

"Cole." She took a deep breath and sat up.

"Yeah."

"We really need to talk."

"I know." A rush of air left his mouth before he stood. "I think I need a beer before we get started on this."

She chuckled. "Bring me one, too, would you?"

He returned a moment later, a beer in both hands. Handing her one, he slid back onto the couch next to her. She took a sip, avoiding looking into his eyes and knowing if they didn't talk now, they wouldn't for a while. She needed to get some things out in the open and find out exactly what his purpose in her life might be.

Taking a deep breath, she asked, "Why did you come back?" *There. It was out.*

"I'm not sure, Carrie." His shoulder lifted in a shrug while he picked at the label on the bottle in his hand. "I wanted to see you again. I know that much. I missed you."

"You didn't even call for six months, then all of the sudden you wanted to see me again? Or was it you were lonely."

A dry chuckle warbled from between his lips when he looked up. "If I just wanted a quick lay, I didn't have to drive twelve hours and almost put myself in the ditch to get it."

"So—why then? You could have called."

"I didn't have your number."

"You didn't ask, either." She stood and started to pace. "You could have called information. It's not like you didn't know the name of the store."

Raking his hands through his hair, he set the bottle on the coffee table. "I know and there's no excuse, but you know you could have called me, too." The defensiveness of his words and the frown on his face told her she fought what was happening between them, too.

But he was right, she could have called, should have probably, but she didn't.

Her heart whispered, you know exactly why you didn't try to call him. It was supposed to be a quick, weekend fling, but your heart got too involved. It was easier to think he walked away than to realize you are in love with him.

She scowled and swirled the beer inside the bottle before she lifted it to her lips. "I was raised the old-fashioned way. Women don't call men, the men call the women." *What a crock of shit that was.*

He stood and walked toward her with a purposeful stride and stopped close enough her nipples almost brushed his muscled pecs. Apprehension skittered down her back when he looked into her eyes and said, "Is that so?"

Shit! He's not buying this.

"Yes." The musk of his cologne and all sexy male surrounded her. *Breathe. Deep slow breaths.*

His intoxicating scent whisked through her brain, and she fought the urge to lock her lips with his. *Bad idea.*

"Then why did you come and find me at the rodeo if the man was supposed to make the first move?" He pressed closer and her heart sped up, slamming against her ribs.

"I…uh."

"Come on, Carrie. Why did you want to find me if you didn't want to hook up?" His breath whispered across her lips, and she almost whimpered before she bit the inside of her mouth to forestall the sound.

"All right. I wanted to find you."

"Why?"

"Because I wanted to say thank you for helping me at the store. It's not every day a stranger helps me." *Yeah. That sounded good.*

"Then why did you let me make love to you?" A hooded gaze bored into hers, and her breath hitched in her throat.

His mouth hovered over hers. If she leaned into him, their lips would touch. Her heart warred with her mind and the needs of her body.

I want him to make love to me and make me forget the horrors of the day. I need to lose myself in his strong arms and let him take away the pain in my heart even for only a few moments, but if I do, I'll lose my heart.

She couldn't breathe—could hardly think clearly when he was this close. The combination of his nearness, his scent, and the need to find comfort in his arms over the loss of her sister loosened her tongue, but her head overruled it at the moment. The first thing that came to her mind sounded snarky, even to her, but she couldn't let him get any closer. "I hadn't been with a man in a very long time. You were the most available."

He stepped back as if he had been slapped while his eyes widened in shock. "That's all it was to you?"

Nonchalant. I need to make him think I don't care. "Yeah. I mean it was just a weekend fling, you know. I told you, I didn't have time for anything permanent in my life, and you said you weren't the settlin' kind, if I remember correctly. You made it perfectly clear you were only here for the weekend."

Tears burned the back of her eyes when she walked away and turned her back on him. A moment later, he grabbed her arm and spun her back around before his mouth swooped down and captured hers. The frustration in his kiss melted her resolve to keep him at arm's length until he left.

I can't do this. I can't push him away when I need him so badly to make me forget right now.

Her nipple hardened beneath his touch when his palm rasped over her breast. Wanting him so badly she ached, she grasped the back of his dress shirt and tugged it from the waistband of his trousers. She slipped her hands under the bottom to feel his warm skin. His lips left hers to quickly unbutton the material while the heat in his eyes scorched her to her soul. He jerked the silky fabric off his arms and dropped it to the floor. Saliva pooled inside her mouth, and she licked her lips, before they met the muscles of his chest and a groan rumbled deep inside him.

In his haste to get her undressed, he grabbed her blouse at the front buttons and pulled so hard they popped off in several different directions.

His belt buckle gave way with a quick flick of her fingers. She quickly unbuttoned his pants and shoved them down his thighs along with his boxers. The skirt she wore gave to the insistent trail of his hands. His boots and her high-heeled shoes went flying as they fell across the couch in a tangle of arms and legs. Soft lips and the titillating feel of whiskers slid across her skin to her breast before he sucked, nipped, and licked until she arched her back.

A callused palm moved down her stomach until his fingers wound in the curls between her thighs. A tortured moan and several whimpers left her lips when they slipped across her clit to between her labia. Two digits dove inside knuckle deep while slick cream spilled from her pussy. Her head tossed on the leather surface while she groaned her passion in loud whispers. She begged and pleaded for him to fuck her, but he continued his slow torture. He spread her open before his mouth moved down and his tongue finally rasped against her clit. "God, Cole—please."

Licking against her swollen center, she could feel the warm liquid spill from her depths only to have him lap it up like a kitten drinking cream. When his fingers slipped inside her while he sucked her hard nub, she lost control and climaxed, screaming his name.

As the world righted itself, he slid back up her body and took her mouth with his. The tip of his cock pressed intimately against her when she lifted her hips. He slid inside with a deep growl that rattled in his chest. Wrapping her legs around his back, he started to move, bringing her to the brink of insanity again.

"I missed you," he growled, letting his pelvis pound into hers.

She whimpered, not daring to say what was on the tip of her tongue, but her heart screamed, *I love you.*

"Do you want to come again?" His thrusts slowed while he waited for her answer.

"Oh, God, yessss…."

She groaned, lifting her hips as far as she could and begging him with her eyes. His groin slapped against hers hard and fast. She started to contract around him, and he moaned above her, riding her, bringing her with him when he growled her name.

"Come with me, Carrie." He buried his nose in her neck and spilled his seed deep in her womb, flooding her with his warmth.

"Oh, God!" she screamed when her climax hit her like the waves crashing against the ragged rocks on the shores of the ocean.

Chapter Twelve

The wail of a baby brought them back to the reality surrounding them.

"Get off."

He groaned and slipped from her warmth but didn't move completely until she pushed against his chest. "Get off. The baby is crying."

Finally lifting himself up, he stared down into her eyes, but she wouldn't look at him until he forced her to. "Don't shut me out, baby."

"I need to take care of Robert."

With a heavy sigh, he rolled off. She sprang to her feet, grabbed her clothes, and slipped them on before she headed for the stairs. She stopped at the bottom, shot him a glance, and then took them two at a time.

Reaching over, he grabbed his jeans and slipped them back up around his waist before snatching the bottle of beer from the table and downing the remainder.

The baby quieted above him, and Carrie's soft voice drifted down to him. His heart clenched, and his stomach flipped over.

What the hell am I doing here? Playing house with a woman who doesn't want me around, fathering a baby that doesn't belong to either of us?

He ran his fingers through his hair and glanced at the empty stairs, before he shook his head.

Moving toward the kitchen, he grabbed another beer, twisted the cap off, and took a long drink. It was almost dinnertime, and Carrie hadn't come back downstairs. Neighbors and friends brought food, lots of food. Crockpots, pans, bowls, and every imaginable type of Tupperware container littered the counters, refrigerator, and sideboard near the window.

Might as well make myself useful.

He lifted the beer to his lips and took another drink. The cabinet near his head opened with a slight tug before he retrieved a couple of plates and dished up some of a wonderful smelling casserole.

"What are you doing?"

He turned when he heard her voice and gave her a thoughtful look. "Making dinner. What's it look like?"

She closed her eyes and shook her head. "Listen, Cole."

"Don't, Carrie. Okay?" He didn't want to fight with her. "It's been a rough day, and we're both tired and cranky. I don't want to fight with you anymore."

"I didn't think we were fighting."

"Disagreeing on who made the first move and why?"

"Okay, maybe we were arguing a little, but what happened afterwards wasn't arguing. It was more like having sex."

"Making love," he countered.

"All right—making love. It shouldn't have happened."

"Why not? It's not like we didn't both want to. I didn't hear you complaining." He let his gaze move from her eyes to her bare toes. "In fact, I think it was more like we both couldn't wait to get our hands on each other. I know I've wanted to since I got back into town, but with everything that's happened. It's didn't feel right before."

"It doesn't matter." She shook her head. "In a few days, you'll leave and…"

He moved to her side and put his finger under her chin, forcing her to look him in the eye. "And what, Carrie?"

She clamped her mouth shut.

"Tell me."

She shook her head.

He bent his head, sliding his tongue along the crease of her lips. She shivered, almost letting out a whimper that she had trapped in her throat, but he heard it anyway. He stepped closer and let his mouth trail across her cheek to her ear, nibbling on her earlobe while she unconsciously moved to give him better access to her neck. Nuzzling her shirt aside with his nose, his lips found the hollow at her collarbone. Stroking the spot with his tongue, she finally gave in and sighed, leaning toward him. His hand found her breast and slid his palm across the nipple while she sucked in a ragged breath. She couldn't deny her body's reaction to his touch.

He dove for the button at her waist, wanting to feel her heat. Slipping it free, his hand moved inside, and his fingers found her clit. Her hands twisted the T-shirt spread across his chest, bunching the material in her fists as she moaned in his mouth.

Removing his hand, he backed her up with his body until her legs touched the dining room table. He lifted her slightly until her butt rested on the top, her legs open for him, and he stepped between them. Grinding his jean-clad cock against her, he felt her shiver at his touch. His hand worked the buttons on the front of her blouse loose while his mouth followed their path. She arched her back and grasped the back of his head, holding him tighter when his lips brushed against her nipple.

"Oh, God," she whispered, tossing her head back, letting her hair trail down her back.

His tongue licked her, and his teeth nibbled the skin beneath his mouth. "I love the way you smell."

Pushing her back so she was lying across the table, he worked his way back down her chest and flicked the button at her waist free. His tongue stopped at her belly button to lave at the indentation before moving lower. He tugged until her jeans slipped down her thighs and off her feet. His lips found the arch of her foot, then her ankle, as he worked his way to her knee. He licked the inside of her thigh, nipping the soft skin and soothing it with his tongue. A high pitched squeal left her lips, and her thighs quivered when he slid his tongue inside her, before sliding across her labia and sucking on her clit.

She panted, "Oh, God—Oh, God," when he alternated with flicking his tongue over her swollen center and sucking it deep into his mouth. He slipped his fingers into her wet pussy and curved them up under her pelvic bone to stroke her G spot. She quivered and contracted around him until her sweet liquid seeped from her center, flooding his mouth.

As she came down from her high, he kissed his way back up her body, settling on her lips. He shucked his pants quickly and then pushed inside her with a tortured groan rumbling in his chest. "God, you feel so good. I can't get enough of you."

His hips rocked, sliding his hard length inside her when she slipped her legs around his hips and hung on. He lifted his chest and watched her eyes close slowly as she got closer and closer to the edge again. Letting his gaze wander down her body to rest between them, he was fascinated by how their bodies fit together so perfectly. When his eyes met hers, he realized she watched their joining, too, and the same look was written on her face.

A low growl ripped from his throat before his mouth swooped down, latching on to hers in almost desperation. His pelvis slapped against hers while their moans mingled. He drove into her, faster and faster, until she clenched around his cock and shouted, "Cole!"

* * * *

Silence surrounded them. She was surprised he couldn't hear her heart shattering when a sob escaped her lips. He lifted his gaze to hers when she dropped her legs, and the confusion on his face made her feel like shit.

All I'm doing is sending mixed signals. It's no wonder he's confused.

When he slipped his cock from her body with a hearty groan, her cheeks flushed with embarrassment. He stepped back and pulled up his jeans, the buckle on his belt tinkling loud in the room. Scrambling from the table, she grabbed her clothes and pulled them on, trying to cover herself from his piercing gaze. She pushed her hair out of her face before turning to meet his stare.

Clasping her hands in front of her in an attempt to stop them from shaking, she couldn't look him in the eye. Focusing on a spot just over his shoulder, she said, "I think you need to leave."

Surprise registered in his eyes, and frown lines settled between his eyebrows. "If that's what you really want."

Tears burned the back of her eyelids. She had to say it.

Tell him, her head screamed. *Tell him to leave because eventually he will, anyway, and the longer he's here, the harder it will be when he does.*

She couldn't say it. A quick nod of her head was the best she could do.

"Fine. I'll get my stuff."

He walked out of the kitchen, and she choked back a sob. She could hear him upstairs as he banged and slammed things. Praying he didn't wake the baby, she just listened, her heart breaking with each sound. When he was finished, she stood by the couch while he approached the door. He stopped and looked at her one last time, before he pulled it open and walked out, shutting it softly behind him.

His truck back out of the driveway while tears rolled down her cheeks and heart-wrenching sobs shook her frame. She sank down on the couch, her face buried in her hands while she rocked back and forth, trying desperately not to shatter with the pain.

* * * *

"Damn it!" He hit the steering wheel with his fist as his truck rolled down the street, plowing through the snow. Raking his fingers through his hair, he wasn't sure what to do now. The last several days had been wrapped around Carrie and baby, but now he just felt lost. "How could she just tell me to leave? Doesn't she know how I feel about her?" He sighed.

How would she know? I've never told her anything. As far as she's concerned, I'm still just here for the short term.

"Time. I just need to give her some time, that's all." The bright neon sign of a Motel Six caught his attention, and he pulled into the driveway. He needed a place to stay, at least for tonight—at least until he could talk to her again and maybe they could get some things straightened out.

Leaving his duffle bag on the seat, he pushed open the door and shivered when the biting wind hit him in the face. Hurrying into the lobby of the motel, he asked for a single room and signed his name to the receipt. Grabbing the key, he headed back for his truck and his lonely bed.

Two hours later, he rolled over and groaned when the jingle of his cell phone dragged him from the exhausted sleep. Blinking in an attempt to focus his eyes, he brought the still ringing phone up to see who it was. He frowned a moment before he flipped it open.

"Chase?"

"Cole, where are you?"

"In Silver Ridge, why?"

"You need to come home. It's Mom. She's had a stroke."

"Shit!" He groaned. "Okay. I'll be there as quick as I can. It'll take me several hours to get home though."

"I know. Be careful, okay? The roads aren't great."

"I will. I'll call you when I get close. Where is she?"

"Still at the hospital."

"Okay. I'll see you in a few hours."

The click of the phone sounded menacing, like someone had just sliced his heart in half. He wanted to be with Carrie, needed to get things straightened out, but his mother needed him at home.

Struggling from the bed, he threw what little he'd taken out the night before back into his bag.

He picked up his phone to call her. "Shit. I still don't have her damn number!" He paced the floor a minute before he dialed information and asked for the number to Marsh's Feed. His heart clenched when he heard Carrie's voice pick up, but it was just the answering machine. When her message was finished, he said, "Carrie, it's me Cole. I realize now that I don't have your home number or cell number, but we need to talk. Call me when you get this okay? My number   is   three-zero-seven-four-two-nine-four-three-zero-eight. There's an emergency at home, so I have to head back there. Please, baby—call me. Talk to you soon."

He closed the phone and held it in his palm for a moment. Shaking his head, he picked up his duffle, opened the motel room door, and let it slam behind him.

The ride back to Laramie was hell. He tried listening to the radio, planning where he would go for the first ride of the season, anything to get his mind off Carrie, but nothing worked. The store would be open already this morning, so she should have gotten his message. He frowned.

Why didn't she call? I could call the store and see if I get her, but knowing her, she'd probably just hang up on me.

The day dragged by while he made his way toward home. When the lights of Laramie finally came into view in the distance, he continued to pick his way along the highway toward the hospital. It was slow going. The roads were slick and covered with snow.

Both the snow plow and Cole stopped at a four-way intersection for a moment before the plow went on through. Cole stopped and looked, but the snow was coming down so hard, it obliterated most of his view. He didn't see anything coming in either direction. The tires spun on the icy snow when he pulled out slowly. His truck fishtailed slightly before grabbing on. He never saw the other vehicle before it broadsided him, knocking his truck into another vehicle sitting at the intersection.

After several minutes, he slowly opened his eyes. His head hurt, and his vision blurred as he tried to focus. The windshield looked like a giant spider web with big chunks missing. His chest burned when he tried to take a deep breath. He brought his hand up to his forehead above his left eye where it hurt, but his fingers came away with blood smeared on them. Pressing his hand against the burning in his side, he groaned and fought for consciousness. He lost the battle and slipped back into oblivion with Carrie's name on his lips.

Chapter Thirteen

Abby and Chase sat in a couple of small chairs in his mother's room at the hospital, talking softly, while Chase's father, Charles, reprimanded his mother, Bonnie, for doing too much. The pad of Chase's thumb rubbed against her hand where their fingers were interlaced. She knew in her heart his mother would be all right although she would have some trouble with movement for the rest of her life. Thank God she was alive. Abby had grown very fond of her mother-in-law, and the last thing she wanted was for Chase to lose her.

Chase's sister, Jamie, had been by earlier to see her mother but had to be home to care for her daughter, Samantha, when she returned from school for the day. Abby smiled when she thought of Jamie. She had seen what the future held for her sister-in-law to a small degree, and Abby knew Jamie would find happiness again—soon.

Abby lost focus on the world around her as her head began to pound with a splitting headache. She involuntarily squeezed Chase's hand and closed her eyes.

"Sweetheart, what's wrong?"

When she opened them again, she tried to smile to reassure her husband. "I'm fine, Chase. I just have a really bad headache."

"Should we go home?"

"No, I'm fine. We need to stay here until Cole gets here."

"Are you sure you are okay? Your face is really pale. You've been doing too much being pregnant and all."

"You are being an overprotective husband and expectant father."

"I love you. Why wouldn't I be?"

Rubbing the soreness clinging just above her left eyebrow, she squeezed his hand as the radio at his waist crackled. She smiled, trying to reassure him, but the pounding in her head kept increasing.

"Accident on the corner of Sheridan Street and Highway Two-eighty-seven. Probably injuries—possible extraction."

Abby gasped and pressed her palm against the spot on her forehand. Feeling very lightheaded and dizzy, she wanted to Chase to understand she was okay, but the pain got worse until a scene flashed behind her eyelids. She moaned when the pain shot through her entire head, and she could vaguely hear Chase calling her name. Tears rolled down her cheeks when she raised her eyes to his.

"Chase—God, Chase, it's Cole. He's hurt."

"What? Where?"

"The accident they just called. It's Cole. You need to help him. He's hurt bad."

"Are you all right?"

"I'm fine, I'll be fine. Just go."

"I love you, Abby. I'll be back as soon as I can."

"I love you, too. Be careful." He kissed her quickly, grabbed his coat, and was gone.

Abby sat on the chair shaking. Her head hurt and now her chest began to burn. She wasn't alarmed at the pain she felt. She knew it all had to do with Cole and where his injuries were. He was alive, that much she knew, but he hovered on the outside watching and trying to communicate. She could hear him whispering. Shaking her head, she tried to clear her thoughts so she could make out what he was saying. She tried reaching him with her mind.

Cole—talk to me.

Silence.

Come on, Cole—talk to me. Tell me.

After a moment, her eyes flew open, and she gasped, startling Bonnie and Charles.

"Something wrong, Abby?" Bonnie asked.

"No." Taking deep, rapid breaths, she tried to calm her heart. Cole's mind reached out to her, but the only thing she could make out were two words—Carrie Marsh.

* * * *

She felt like shit. Crying all night and then needing to be up every four hours to feed the baby drew the last of her energy, and she still had to open the store. Thank the Lord for Agnes, her next-door neighbor. She willingly offered to babysit Jess's son while Carrie worked the store today.

Pulling the door open, she somehow managed to get ready for the first customers just in time. The snow had let up some, and the store was hopping. Several people had run out of feed during the weeklong snow.

Her eyes misted over when her thoughts turned to Jess. The sun had shone bright the other day when they buried her, but now the clouds returned, enveloping her heart in sadness. She lost her parents, she lost her sister, and now she lost Cole, too. She was all alone except for the baby.

The blinking light on the answering machine caught her eye when she had come into the office this morning, but the steady stream of customers prevented her from finding out who called. "It was probably a customer who came in, anyway." It was five, and she was never so thankful for it to be closing time.

Finding her employee in the back room, she asked, "Mark? Can you lock the front?"

"Sure, Carrie."

She grabbed the cash from the register and headed to the office to put everything away.

"You need anything else before I go?"

"No, thanks. I'm good. I'm just going to lock everything down and head for home."

"See you tomorrow, then."

"Sure. Night, Mark."

She glanced at the answering machine and hit the button to listen while she slipped the cash bag into the safe. Her heart skipped a beat when she heard Cole's voice. Tears gathered on her lashes as he said, "Please, baby—call me." She played back the message again, jotting down the number. She wasn't sure she would call him, but she wanted it, anyway, just in case.

Carrie made her way to the door, shutting off the lights as she went. The phone rang, but she ignored it until she heard a female voice, one she didn't recognize.

"Carrie? If this is Carrie Marsh's phone and you can hear me, pick up the phone, please." The desperation rang clearly in the woman's voice.

Silence.

"Carrie, please, if you can hear me, pick up the phone. My name is Abby Wilder. I'm Chase's wife and I need to talk to you. It's an emergency. It's Cole."

Her breath caught in her throat for a moment as she raced for the office and grabbed the phone.

"Hello?"

"Carrie?"

"Yes."

"Oh, thank the Lord I got you. This is the only number I could find."

"What's wrong? What about Cole?"

"There was a terrible accident. He's hurt, Carrie, and we don't know if he'll make it or not. There is a lot of damage."

"Oh, God..." she whispered, pressing her fingers to her lips when she remembered his desperate kisses from the night before.

"He needs you, Carrie. Please. You have to come to Laramie."

"I don't know. I mean we didn't part on the best of terms."

"It doesn't matter right now. He needs you here."

Silence.

"Carrie, I don't know if Cole told you about me, but I can see things and know things."

"No, not really."

"I can and, Carrie? I don't want to scare you, and I haven't even told his family, but if you don't come, he'll die."

"But I…"

"He loves you, Carrie. He may not even know it yet himself, but he does. He needs your strength and your love to heal."

"I don't…"

"Don't tell me you don't love him because I know you do. I can feel it through the phone."

Sobs racked her frame and tears rolled down her face. "All right. I'll be there as quick as I can. Can someone pick me up at the airport? That's the fastest way for me to get there. I have to pack some things for me and the baby. I'll call you from the airport."

"Baby?"

"It's not Cole's. He's my nephew."

"Ah. By the way, I wasn't judging."

"It's okay. I'll call you back in a little bit. Give me a number I can reach you." She jotted down the number and said, "Thanks for calling me, Abby."

"You have no idea how much your presence here is needed. I'll see you shortly."

She hung up the phone, racing for the door before she slammed it shut and ran for her truck.

Be careful, she thought. *It won't do him any good if I get hurt trying to get there.*

Picking up the baby from her neighbor, she hurried to the house, threw some clothing for both of them in a bag, and sat down to call the airport. Luckily, there was one more flight that night for Laramie. She booked it, grabbed her bags, and headed for the truck. Not having a lot of time before the flight left, she tried to get there as quickly as possible. Once she was checked in, she found a chair and called Abby.

"How is he?"

"He's still unconscious, but he's hanging in there for now."

She told Abby what time the flight was due in and hung up. The tears started to well up in her eyes again as she sent up a silent prayer for God not to take him from her, too.

Boarding the flight, she settled herself into a seat and strapped the baby into his car seat next to her. Luckily, the flight wasn't full.

It didn't take long for them to reach Laramie, and when the plane rolled into the gate, she called Abby back to let her know they were there.

"Great. I'll meet you out front, then."

She chuckled. "I'll be the haggard looking one toting a baby."

Abby laughed, too. "I'm sure I'll be able to find you then."

A nice looking cowboy helped her take her luggage out to the curb. He was polite, tall, with dark hair and brown eyes, but he wasn't Cole.

"Thank you for helping me."

"You're welcome, ma'am." He tipped his hat with a twinkle in his gaze.

"Thanks."

She heard a female's voice behind her say her name, and when she turned around, she wasn't the least bit surprised to be wrapped in a warm hug. "Abby?"

Abby stepped back. "Yeah." She took in Carrie's appearance with one sweep, and Carrie knew she looked like hell.

"Come with me. You could use a nice bath, about twenty-four hours of sleep and someone to talk to, I'm sure."

Carrie choked back a sob and nodded before she picked up Robert and they walked out to Abby's truck.

"When's your baby due?"

Abby laid her hand across her stomach and smiled. "In about four more months."

"I'm happy for you. I'm sure you'll be a wonderful mom."

"Thanks. You look like you are doing pretty well yourself."

"Yeah, well—looks are deceiving. I'm trying, though. I didn't have a lot of training on this."

Abby laughed. "I don't think any of us do."

Carrie smiled but dropped her gaze.

"I'm sorry for your loss."

"It's okay. I'm sure it's going to hurt for a long time to come."

"It's not easy losing a loved one."

Carrie peeked at Abby through her lashes, wondering at the sad smile that lingered on her lips. Her attention was drawn away when the ranch came into view.

When they pulled into the driveway in front of the house, a man whom she assumed was Cole's brother came out and opened the door. "Hi there. You must be Carrie."

"Yes, I am. Chase?" When Chase nodded, she continued, "Cole's told me about you."

"Uh-oh. That can't be good. Whatever he said, I'm sure most of it is a lie."

She let a small smile lift the corners of her mouth. "Not bad things, honest, but I can certainly see the resemblance, especially the dimples."

Abby curled her arm around her husband's waist. "I know. I just love them, don't you?"

Chase chuckled, but she could still see the strain on his face. "I'm going to like you, Carrie. I'm just terrified at the trouble you and Abby will get in."

Abby playfully punched him in the side. "You behave yourself, husband. Don't go scaring her off already."

"Me?"

Carrie grabbed the baby seat and Chase gave her a questioning raise of his eyebrow.

Abby whispered in his ear, "I'll explain later and no, you aren't an uncle, at least not yet."

He physically relaxed and Carrie felt heat fuse her cheeks.

They showed her into the house, giving her Cole's room for her and the baby. "Can I help you with anything?" Abby asked.

"No. I'm fine. I need a minute alone to kind of wrap my mind around this."

"Sure." Abby hugged her and then left the room. She took in his space as her gaze wandered around the room. It didn't look very lived in—kind of like he was only there temporarily. *Just like at my house.* She walked to the bed and pulled the pillow to her face. It didn't smell like him. It just smelled like laundry soap. She put her things in one of the empty dresser drawers, changed the baby, and walked back into the living room.

Abby and Chase were sitting on the couch, snuggled together, and she laid her head on his lap. Carrie sighed. She wanted that so badly. She ached for it.

Her heavy sigh brought the attention of the couple, and Abby sat up with a groan.

"Can we go to the hospital now? I need to see him."

"Of course. Let's get everyone packed in the truck and we'll go. It's not far."

When they were all settled and on their way, Carrie asked, "Why did he come home anyway? He was just at my house the night before." She remembered the argument they had and how she told him to leave while pain ripped across her heart.

"I called him. Our mother had a stroke, and he came home to be here for her."

"Oh, my. I'm sorry. I didn't realize."

"It's okay. She's doing much better although she is upset that he is there now."

"I can only imagine," Carrie whispered.

They rolled into the hospital parking lot and walked inside, headed for the elevator. The next floor up held the intensive care unit.

"You won't be able to take the baby in there, but I'll be happy to watch him for you."

"Thanks, Abby."

"Come with me. I'll take you inside," Chase said as he took her hand in his.

Her heart began to pound in terror. She wasn't sure what she would find when she got inside, but she was scared.

What if he never recovers? Will he even want to see me?

"You have to be prepared, Carrie. He's on a ventilator to help him breathe. One of his lungs collapsed and he has chest tubes in. There are lots of tubes and wires, but remember, he is doing okay—for now."

A sob slipped from between her lips. *A ventilator? Oh my God!*

They walked together toward the glass door. Chase put his arm around her shoulder, and she was thankful for his support. As she stepped into the room, she could hear the beeping of the machine and see all the tubes and wires coming out of his body. It didn't even look like him.

It's a mistake! It has to be!

"It's okay, Carrie."

Chase walked with her to Cole's side, and tears rolled down her cheeks. She took his hand in hers right before she felt a chair touch the back of her legs before Chase forced her to sit down.

"They say people in a coma can hear when you talk to them. Talk, Carrie. He needs to know you're here."

She choked back a sob and brought his hand to her cheek.

"Cole?" She looked up at his face as she ran her hand up his arm. His long lashes lay softly against his cheek, shielding his piercing blue eyes from her. The tube coming from his mouth scared her, but she could feel his heartbeat against her palm and see it on the screen above his head. He was still so warm even if his hand lay flaccid in hers. "It's me, Carrie. Abby called me and told me you were here. I had to come." A sob left her lips. "I just can't leave you alone for a minute, can I? Always in trouble." Smiling softly, she said, "I brought Robert with me. I can't bring him in here, though. I know you would like to see him, but you will have to get better so you can."

Someone behind them cleared their throat. "I'm sorry, but visiting hours are over."

"Okay," she whispered, her eyes never leaving the man in the bed. "I'll be back in the morning. I'm staying with Chase and Abby. I'll be here as long as you need me to be."

She stood up and leaned over the bed, placing a small kiss to his cheek while tears rolled down her face.

"I need you so much. Don't leave me, too."

Chapter Fourteen

Abby insisted Carrie let her take the baby and take care of him for the night while she got some sleep. Carrie stretched her muscles, her arms over her head, trying to relieve the aches and pains that she was beginning to think were a permanent part of her.

Grabbing her robe, she slipped it on and cinched it tight at her waist. The smell of coffee and bacon reached her nose, making her mouth water, and she realized she hadn't eaten since the day before at lunch.

She walked into the living room to find Abby sitting on the couch, feeding the baby a bottle while Chase cooked breakfast. She had to smile. Obviously their mother made sure her sons knew how to cook.

"Well, good morning. Sleep well?" Abby asked.

"It was heavenly. I hope he wasn't too much trouble for you last night."

"Of course not. He is an angel," Abby said, snuggling the precious little bundle to her and moving toward the table.

Abby didn't see the surprised expression her husband's face from the kitchen, and Carrie almost burst out laughing. Obviously Chase didn't share the sentiment.

"Would you like some coffee?"

"Yes, thank you."

Chase poured her a cup and one for Abby, setting them on the dining room table. "Breakfast will be ready in a bit."

"Thanks, sweetie," Abby said while Chase nibbled at her neck for a moment before returning to the food. Carrie dropped her gaze from the affectionate display, and her heart clenched when she wondered if Cole would ever do that to her again.

"Let me go change him really fast. Carrie, why don't you go ahead and eat. I'm sure you are anxious to get back to the hospital."

"Yeah—actually I am."

Abby flashed a secretive smile before heading for what Carrie assumed was their bedroom.

Taking a seat at the table, her gaze shifted to the man in the kitchen. Family meant everything to her these days and she wanted to meet all of Cole's siblings and get to know them. It would be interesting to see how different the brothers were from each other.

Getting involved with his family isn't conducive to keeping my heart from shattering. She frowned. *Who am I kidding, anyway? I can't but help being in love with that stubborn man lying in the bed at the hospital, but the question is, am I going to let him hurt me?*

Abby returned a few minutes later, placed the baby in his seat while he drifted off to sleep and sat down to eat her own breakfast. She took Carrie's hand in hers for a moment. "Don't let him walk away, Carrie. He cares about you, even if he won't admit it."

"What? How did you…?"

Chase chuckled from her side when he placed the plate in front of Abby. "You'll get used to it. She does that all the time." He put his hand on Abby's shoulder, giving it a gentle squeeze.

Carrie's gaze ricocheted to the doorway when another very handsome man moved into the living room. She tilted her head slightly while she took in the fact that he wore no shirt and only a pair of Wranglers that hugged his muscular thighs like a second skin. His broad chest had a smattering of brown hair displayed across the finely sculpted muscles that only came from hard, physical labor. She followed the fine line of hair until it disappeared into the waistband of the jeans, which rode on his hips.

She blushed when her eyes met his, and he cocked an eyebrow in her direction before a small smile swept across his lips. It was one of those smiles whispering he was all virile male and knew she watched him.

"It's about time you got up," Chase shot over his shoulder.

"I've been up for a while now." The deep, gravelly voice made the hair on her arms stand up. "You know me. I'm usually up with the chickens. Besides, I heard the strangest noise most of the night—a baby crying off and on."

"Sorry. I tried keeping him quiet," Abby replied.

"No big deal, Abby. It's not a sound I expected to hear, knowing you still have several months before you deliver."

His gaze connected with Carrie's again before it traveled from her head to her toes. Once he was finished with his once over, he walked into the kitchen and poured a cup of coffee. He turned and braced against the counter top before he brought the cup to his lips, watching her over the rim.

"Sorry. I guess I should introduce you two. Justin, this is Carrie Marsh. She's a…uh…friend of Cole's. Carrie, this is my older brother Justin."

"It's nice to meet you," she managed to say without too much difficulty although she thought her voice sounded rather low and whispery.

"Likewise." He smiled, flashing the same dimples that were evident in all three brothers.

"Sorry about the baby. Abby offered to help me with him."

With a questioning cock of his eyebrow he said, "He's yours?"

"Yes…I mean, no, not really." He shot a confused look at Chase and she could almost see the wheels spinning. "He's my nephew, but I'm responsible for him now."

"Ah. Sorry. Didn't mean anything by it."

"It's okay. We always get that reaction, especially when people know Cole and I are friends. They immediately think Cole is the father."

He took the plate of food from Chase and slipped onto the seat next to her. "So, Carrie Marsh, what brings you to Laramie?"

"Your brother."

* * * *

An hour later found Carrie standing in the doorway of Cole's room. Chewing her bottom lip, she slowly approached his side and pulled up a chair. Taking his hand in hers, she ran her fingers over the top for a moment.

"I don't know if you can hear me or not." She looked up at the ceiling, trying to hold back the tears. "I wanted you to know I'm here though." She scooted closer. "I'm sorry things ended the way they did the other night. I should never have made you leave, but I'm scared, Cole. Here you are in this bed, and I don't know if you are going to be okay or not." Hot tears rolled down her cheeks, dropping onto the top of his hand. "What am I going to do if I lose you too? I can't do that again, Cole, I just can't. It was easier for me to push you away than to let you hurt me by leaving."

A sob shook her frame when she rested his hand against her cheek. "I can't fight what I feel anymore. If it means opening myself up for you to hurt me, then I guess that's what happens. I pray that you don't, and I pray hard that God doesn't take you from me like he took my parents and Jess. I don't think I could bear it if you left me too." She stood up and kissed him softly on the cheek before she whispered in his ear. "I love you."

Startled, she looked up. His eyes were still closed, and the machine still breathed for him, but she was sure she felt the small brush of his fingers as they moved against her hand. A soft smile flittered across her lips, and she kissed him again.

"I better go now. I know your family wants to come in for a little bit. I'll see you later today."

Slipping from his side, she took one last look before she slowly walked out to the waiting area where she left Chase and Abby. She was startled to see a very elegant lady and one mildly haggard gentleman sitting next to the other couple as well as one twenty-something young woman with a little girl tucked to her side. Her heart sped up as Chase stood and reached her side, pulling her along until she came to stand near them.

"Carrie, I'd like you to meet someone. These are our parents, Bonnie and Charles Wilder—and those two there are our sister, Jamie, and my niece, Samantha."

"It's nice to meet you."

This is who your father came to see all those years in Laramie. This is the woman your mother hated and cursed with every breath she took until the day she died.

"Mom—Dad, this is Carrie Marsh. She's a friend of Cole's."

The two older people exchanged a strange look before their gazes came back to her, and she wondered if they would reveal the connection of their families or keep their silence. "You are Josephine and Allen's daughter?"

"Yes."

Bonnie held out her hand, and Carrie was terrified to take it.

How can I be friendly to these two? This woman's connection to my father was enough to almost tear my parent's marriage in two, and now she wants to be friendly?

Bonnie frowned. "Is there something wrong, dear?"

"How could you?" She couldn't keep it inside anymore. All the pain and grief her mother put on Carrie's shoulders, welled up inside her. All the disappointments from the missed birthdays and family gatherings because her father was in Laramie, spilled over in hot tears. "I don't believe you!"

Chase and Justin stood and moved between the two women, protecting their mother.

"Carrie, you need to calm down. I know you are upset about Cole and..."

Her eyes shot up the two men. "She never told you, did she? Never told anyone, I'm sure. God help her if anyone in your nice little community found out she was an adulteress and having an illicit affair with a married man. Well, my mother told me."

"That's enough, Carrie," Justin growled.

"I'm confused. I have no idea what you are talking about," Bonnie answered, shock written all over her face.

"Allen Marsh! He came here several times each year. Even missed birthdays to be with you." Her eyes ricocheted to the stately man next to her. "Did you know? Are any of your children even yours?" Realization hit her square in the face and she slumped in the chair. "Oh, God! I might have had sex with my brother."

Bonnie wheeled the chair to her side. "Carrie, listen to me. Allen and I were never together as a couple. Charles and I were in love from high school, and Allen was our friend. He came here on several occasions to buy livestock and stayed because we were friends. He often talked about your mother. He loved her with all his heart, but she was so jealous she could never see his love for what it was, a gift."

Carrie wasn't sure whom to believe. The woman in front of her had sincerity written on her face and her mother wasn't here to ask. "But she told me..."

"Your mother hated me. She knew how close Allen and I were, but I swear to you, I never felt anything for him except loving him like he was my brother." Bonnie picked up her hand and held it tight. "I prayed so hard for so many nights that your mother would let go of the jealousy she harbored." Bonnie placed her hand against Carrie's cheek. "I wanted so much to be there for you and your sister when they died, but I couldn't. I didn't know she had burdened you with her hatred, but I knew I wouldn't be welcome. I'm sorry I didn't bury my misgivings and come to you."

"I don't know what to think."

"It's okay, sweetheart. I don't expect you to change your feelings for me overnight."

"I'm sorry about what I said. I believed what my mother told me. I knew my father came here all the time for some reason, but he didn't divulge your relationship. The only thing I knew about you was what she told me."

Bonnie reached over and hugged her. "I never knew your mother and father didn't tell you and Jess about us. He talked about all of you so often, I felt like I knew you. He didn't want to cause Bonnie any more hurt. I would assume that's why he didn't mention our friendship." Bonnie smiled wistfully before she patted Carrie's hand and said, "Now, tell me how you know my Cole?"

A watery smile spread across her mouth beneath the tears. She laid out the story of how they met and what had happened between them over the last six months. When she told them of how she made him leave the other night, the same night Chase called him about Bonnie's stroke, tears fell down her cheeks.

"You'll have your chance. He'll be okay now that you are here to help him," Bonnie said, squeezing her hand.

"Excuse me," an older gentleman in a long white lab coat approached from behind.

"Ah, Dr. Collier. How is Cole this morning?"

"He's doing much better. I'm going to take him off the ventilator and I wanted to let you know."

"That's wonderful. When can we see him?"

"Soon. I'll come back down when I know he's able to breathe on his own without too much effort."

"Thank you. We'll wait right here."

Carrie stood and began to pace.

What will he say when he wakes up? Will he be glad to see me or will be tell me to leave?

She rubbed her arms, trying to calm the nervous goose bumps that rose on her skin. She knew his family watched, wondering what was really between them, but she couldn't say anything. Not yet. She had to talk to Cole first.

Two hours later, the doctor returned and told them they could go up and see him. Carrie followed behind the rest of his family, holding back as they reached the door to his room. The machine was gone, but he was still very pale while he lay there with his eyes closed until his mother said his name.

He slowly opened them to her voice. He turned toward her and smiled before he grimaced and groaned.

"Are you in pain?"

"Yeah, just a little." His voice cracked like he hadn't used it in a long time. "The chest tube is killing me, and my throat hurts some."

"I'm sure they'll give you something in a little bit."

"Hey, little brother. You look like shit," Chase stated from the doorway.

"Thanks, Chase. I could always count on you to cheer me up."

They all laughed.

"I just can't leave you and Chase alone, can I? Bad enough I have to keep Jamie in line. Always into something, all three of you," Justin said as he shook his head.

"Like hell, Justin. Big brother or not, stay out of my way and you won't get hurt," Jamie grumbled, and the men laughed again.

Cole frowned. "When did you get here?"

"I came in before you did. Little did I know two of my family would be in this place. You know I hate hospitals."

"We all know your affinity for them, Justin," Cole said.

"Cole, there's someone here to see you." Abby pulled Carrie by the hand and shoved her up next to the bed. At first, his eyes lit up before he frowned.

"What are you doing here?"

Her heart dropped to her toes. *He hates me.* She couldn't say anything as she turned and ran from the room.

* * * *

"If you weren't stuck in that bed right now, I'd kick your ass for you, Cole Wilder," Abby said.

He frowned when his gaze met hers. "What?"

"She came all the way here to see you, and you practically throw her out of the room." Abby glared at him, and he shifted uncomfortably in the bed.

His gaze shifted to the door where Carrie disappeared. *It was pure shock, that's all. I just didn't expect her to be here.* "Find her, Abby. I need to talk to her."

"That's better. I'll do what I can, but with that attitude, I don't know if she'll even come back in here."

"You have to try. I need to tell her something."

When Abby disappeared, his gaze locked with his mother and father. "Mom? Are you okay? I came here to see you, not end up in the bed beside you. What the hell happened anyway?"

"You were t-boned at the corner of Sheridan and two-eighty-seven," Chase explained. "You are hurt pretty badly, but it sounds like you'll recover okay."

"How did Carrie get here?"

"She flew here after Abby called her and told her you had been hurt. She cares about you, Cole. Don't mess that up," Chase told him.

Cole frowned. Something wasn't right.

"Where's the baby?"

"Baby?" The startled look on his mother's face almost made him laugh.

"He's not mine, Mom, so don't get your hopes up. Carrie's sister died a little over a week ago having him. I helped her with him before I came home."

"One of my neighbors is watching him today since we all came to the hospital to see you," Chase answered.

"Jessie's dead?" Bonnie asked with a startled look on her face.

Cole frowned. It almost sounded like his mother knew her. "Yeah."

"Oh my God, Charles. Jessie's gone. No wonder Carrie is so upset."

"Why do I get the feeling you know them?"

"I'll explain it to you later, son, when you are feeling better, but yes, I know them. Well, sort of. Your father and I were good friends of Carrie's father. We never really got to know the girls, although I've seen plenty of pictures of them but nothing recently. I didn't recognize Carrie when Chase introduced us."

Cole looked up at the sound by the door, and his eyes met Carrie's across the room. She had been crying. Her face was puffy, and her eyes were red and swollen. "Carrie. Come here, baby."

She hesitated as her gaze shifted to his family.

"We'll go now so you two can talk. We will see you after while."

He didn't even notice the departure of his family except when Justin's gaze lingered a little longer on Carrie, before he disappeared out the door. He held out his hand, and she slowly walked to his side and slid onto the chair next to the bed. Lifting his hand, he brushed his thumb across her cheek, wiping away the lingering tears.

He smiled. "Hi."

She bit her lip before she answered, "Hi."

"I'm sorry about before. I was just shocked you were here."

"I had to come. When Abby called me...I didn't know what else to do."

"I didn't think you wanted to see me again."

She dropped her gaze to the bed.

"Carrie?"

"I'm sorry. I shouldn't have made you leave."

"I planned to come back over there the next day so we could talk, but I got the phone call from Chase." He linked their fingers together.

"I know. I got your message on the answering machine at the store, but it wasn't until right before Abby called me later."

"And?"

"I need to tell you something. I didn't want you to leave the other night, but I'm scared. You told me from the beginning you weren't the settlin' kind, and I took that to heart. I wanted to push you away before you left on your own, thinking it would hurt less that way. I can't help how I feel. I'll just have to deal with it if you do decide to leave and not come back, but I want whatever you are willing to give me."

"I heard something when I was still out of it, so I don't know for sure if it's true or not."

"What's that?"

"Did you kiss me and tell me you loved me?" She looked away. He took her chin in his hand, forcing her to look at him. "Tell me."

"Yes, I did."

"Say it again."

"I love you."

He sighed. "Good."

"Good?"

"Yeah. If I have to give up my wandering ways, I want to make sure the girl I'm willing to give them up for loves me, too."

"What are you saying?"

"I love you, Carrie. I think I fell in love with you the first time I saw you."

She laughed as tears rolled down her cheeks. "While I stood there yelling at you for getting Jess pregnant? In fact, I think I called you a bastard."

"And a son of a bitch."

"Yeah, that, too."

He smiled and shrugged. "Not like I haven't been called that before." He brushed her tears away "You have no idea how beautiful you were, all protective and ready to take on the world to look after her." He brushed his fingers across her face. "I was a goner as soon as you stuck your claws in me."

"I don't have claws."

"Oh, yes, you do. You were like a lioness defending her young." He pulled her closer. "Now—come here. I need to feel your lips against mine."

She stood up and reached over the railing. "I love you," she whispered, before her lips moved over his. It was the best feeling in the world.

Someone cleared his throat behind them, and she pulled away with a smile.

"I need to check you over, Cole." Dr. Collier walked to his bedside and smiled.

"I'll be back after a while," she whispered.

"I'll count on it. I love you, Carrie."

"I love you, too."

She grabbed her purse and walked toward the door. With a short, backward glance, she headed for the lobby and his family.

Chapter Fifteen

"What are you saying, Dr. Collier?"

"You may never walk again, Cole."

"That can't be right!"

"You can't feel your legs. Your back is fractured and pressing on your spinal column. I can't tell right now if there is permanent damage or not. There is too much swelling to tell."

He raked his fingers through his hair. Looking down at the two bumps beneath the blankets, he concentrated on moving them, but nothing happened.

"Don't worry too much about it right now. Until the swelling goes down, I can't do even do any more tests. It may only be temporary."

He put his head back against the pillow behind him and closed his eyes. *Not walk again?* "Have you said anything to my family?"

"No, I'm headed down to find them now."

"All right."

"Take it easy, Cole. We don't know the extent of the damage yet, so don't do anything rash like try to get up on your own."

He snorted, but didn't open his eyes when he heard the doctor leave.

Now what the hell am I going to do?

Millions of thoughts raced across his mind. He may never be able to ride again, never be able to do much of anything again, including making love to Carrie.

I feel worthless. How can I ask Carrie to spend the rest of her life with me if I can't take care of her?

* * * *

Carrie found the family sitting about where they had been before and she told them the doctor came in to examine Cole. They all agreed to get something to eat to pass the time until they could see him again.

Once they all ordered food in the cafeteria, small talk centered around the horses Chase and Abby were training, the coming baby, and how excited Chase's parents were to become grandparents again.

Several minutes later, Dr. Collier approached their table.

"Bonnie—Charles. Can I talk to you for a moment?"

"Certainly, but whatever you need to say can be said in front of my children. Is this to do with me or with Cole?"

"It's about Cole."

Carrie's heart dropped to her stomach. *Something's wrong.*

The doctor took a chair next to Bonnie and pulled her hand into his.

"Bonnie, there's a problem."

"What, Dr. Collier? Just tell us, all right? We will handle it as a family, like we always have."

He patted her hand before his gaze swept the group and landed on Carrie.

"The accident was pretty hard on him. You know he had a collapsed lung."

"Yes."

"That part is okay now. The chest tube is helping, and we'll probably be able to remove it in a day or so."

"Get to the point."

He sighed. "Cole had an injury to his back. He has a fracture to his spinal column, which basically means he broke his back."

"And?"

"He can't feel his legs."

"He's paralyzed?" Bonnie's gasp was echoed throughout the group.

"Yes."

"Oh, my God," Carrie whispered before her hand covered her mouth.

"I don't know at this point if it's permanent or temporary. I'll have to do some more tests, but for now, he won't be able to walk. Obviously, this means his rodeo days are over. Even if the condition is only temporary, he'll need extensive rehabilitation."

I can't believe what I'm hearing. He can't walk, may never walk again.

She stood up and moved to the window. The snow continued to fall in swirling white crystals, laying a heavy blanket over the streets, buildings, and cars. Christmas was just around the corner, and it was the first one without Jess.

"You okay?" Abby put her arm around Carrie's shoulder.

Her lips quivered and she tried to hold back the sob lingering in her throat. "Not really. God, Abby. What if he never walks again?" Carrie shook her head in denial. "I don't understand how this could happen. He's so strong and is always there for everyone else."

"I know. It's not going to be easy on anyone."

"I need to talk to him, let him know it doesn't matter if he can't walk. I still love him no matter what."

"That would probably be a good thing. If I know Cole at all, he's going to be feeling sorry for himself. Not being able to ride is one thing, but never being able to walk again? That could do some real damage to his male pride."

"Thanks, Abby."

"You're welcome. I'll keep the family down here for a bit."

Carrie hugged Abby before she moved toward the elevator to see the man she loved.

* * * *

"Cole?" Carrie's soft whisper reached his ears right before she touched his hand.

Opening his eyes, he saw her sit down next to him, and she tried to smile. The worry lines around her mouth and between her eyes made her look older than her twenty-six years. He knew with all the crap she had put up with over the last two years, his injuries just added to it.

"Hey. How do you feel?"

"Like shit."

She shook her head, and her fingers caressed his hand.

"Did the doctor talk to y'all?"

"Yeah."

Tears formed at the corners of his eyes and slipped down his cheek as a sob broke from his lips. She stood up and sat on the side of the bed with him, wrapping her arms around his shoulders.

"It's going to be okay," she whispered, holding him tight.

"I can't move my legs, Carrie." He held on. She was his lifeline, his tether in the tornado that his life had become, as the world came crashing down around him.

"I know. It doesn't matter. I love you—all of you." His nose buried in her hair, he inhaled her sweet scent, letting it wrap around his senses and carry him back to when they made love. Just the scent of her and her body next to his should have sent his cock into overdrive, and it terrified him to realize nothing was happening.

They sat that way for several minutes. Hearing sounds coming from the doorway, Carrie released him to move back to the chair. The rest of his family came into the room, and he wiped the tears remaining on his face.

His parents took over, just like they always had. They made plans for him to be moved to their house in town when the doctor released him. He watched as the group time-lined everything out, who would take care of him, how they would hire someone to do extensive rehabilitation and so on. His mind spun from the information and how his family seemed to almost dismiss him from the conversation. He decided to take over. With a shrill whistle he released from between his lips, the room grew silent.

"This is my life and my problem. *I* will figure out what needs to be done." His gaze caught his mother's startled expression. "I love you, Mom, but I'm a big boy now, and I'll make my own arrangements. Nothing has to be settled right this minute, anyway, since I'll be here for several more days from what it sounds like."

"But, Cole…" His mother started to argue, and he raised his hand to silence her protest.

"I'll handle this." His gaze swept the room before landing on his eldest brother, and he frowned when he saw where the other man's eyes settled. "You could probably go ahead and go back to Nevada, Justin, unless Mom needs you here." His brother's brown eyes swung back to his with a shocked expression. "I know you have cattle to take care of."

"That sounds an awful lot like a brush off, little brother."

"No." He drew out the word on several syllables. "I'm thinking of your ranch, that's all."

"Since when are you worried about my place?" Justin stepped closer to the bed and stopped directly behind Carrie.

Cole didn't answer at first. He didn't trust his mouth to say something he would regret later like *"Go the hell home, Justin, and leave Carrie alone."* Finally, he couldn't stay quiet. "Since you've decided to pay an awful lot of attention to *my* girl."

Silence filled the room except a small gasp that escaped Carrie's mouth.

Cole couldn't miss the challenge in his brother's eyes.

He's set his sights on Carrie, and there isn't a damned thing I can do about it.

"Your girl? I don't see a ring on her finger, Cole."

Cole narrowed his eyes to mere slits and growled, "Keep your distance, *brother.*"

Carrie stood and almost shouted, "That's about enough out of both of you. I'm not a piece of meat you two can fight over like two dogs. I'll make up my own mind as to who I'm with—not either of you."

"But, Carrie…"

"Don't you but Carrie me, Cole. I think you would have learned over the period of time you've known me that I'm an independent female if nothing else. I will not allow *any* man to decide my life for me."

"Yeah. I can't deny that." A soft chuckle left his lips. He had almost forgotten how beautiful she was when anger infused her face. The soft flush of color that rose on her cheeks had him shifting in the bed uncomfortably when he felt the stirrings of desire.

Maybe things aren't as bad as they seem.

"Then you should know better. This high-handed behavior will get you nothing." She turned to face Justin. "As for you, I don't even know you, so don't go getting any wild ideas."

"Wouldn't you like to?"

Cole could have spit nails when the soft timbre of his brother's voice drawled the words. Carrie's face turned a deeper red, and his frown deepened when his gaze shifted from her to his brother.

Does she want to get to know Justin better? I thought she said she loved me. It would be just like a woman to say she loved one man and then change her mind a few moments later if offered something better. Besides, what can I offer her? I'm just a drifter—no income now since I can't ride or work on trucks. Justin has the ranch in Nevada. He would be just the type of guy Carrie would be attracted to. She told me once she wasn't interested in a temporary man in her life.

"I should get some rest. I'm kind of tired since they gave me something for pain not long before y'all came in."

"Okay, son. We'll leave you alone," Bonnie replied, heading for the door while the rest of the family followed. Justin shot Cole a challenging look before sliding his glance to Carrie then disappearing.

"I need to get the baby, anyway. He's been with Chase's neighbor all morning. I'll come back later this afternoon." Carrie stepped closer, obviously intending to kiss him goodbye, but he turned his face so her lips brushed his cheek instead. A deep frown marred her face as she moved back.

"That's not necessary, Carrie. I think they are going to do some more tests this afternoon, anyway."

"If that's what you want," she whispered, pain reflected in her eyes.

"That's what I want." He knew he was being stubborn, and the hurt on her face almost made him change his mind.

It would be better to stop this whole thing now, rather than later. She would be better off with Justin, anyway. What good am I to her if I can't walk?

"I love you."

"I'll see you later."

She bit her lip before turning away and walking out his door.

He released a heavy sigh, tipping his head back against the bed.

Chapter Sixteen

"Are you okay, Carrie?" Abby stopped her in the hall not far from Cole's room.

"I guess." She shook her head. "I just don't understand him."

Abby laughed. "Get used to it. That's the way it is with Wilder men, no matter which one you choose. They say women are impossible to understand…"

Carrie couldn't help but smile as she hugged Abby. "I get the feeling we need to sit down and talk before I have to kill one of them, and I'll give you one guess which one."

Abby linked her arm with Carrie's. "That we do. How about we bring the baby and go out tonight so we can talk without the men hearing?"

"I think I like that idea. I could probably use a beer. Is it too early to start drinking?"

"How about later? We can go shopping, though. I still need to get a few things for this little one."

"More shopping? Good grief, woman, we won't have any room in the house at this rate," Chase teased when they approached.

"Oh, hush, daddy. I'm not buying any more clothes and what not, but we still need diapers."

"Good. You've already got one closet full and working on another."

Abby smiled and slid into his arms. Carrie's heart clenched at the sight. She remembered those nights with Cole, and she wanted that again, for the rest of her life. He told her he loved her earlier, and then didn't respond when she said it again before she left the room. She didn't know what to think anymore.

"Don't worry about him, Carrie. He'll come around." Chase's advice mimicked his wife's, but she wasn't so sure. All of the sudden, Cole seemed to be pushing her away, and she wasn't sure she had the energy to fight him anymore.

She shook her head. "I don't know what his problem is now."

"My guess would be he's feeling not quite a man anymore."

"What do you mean, Chase?"

"He can't move his legs, Carrie. What was he doing before this? He rode rodeo—rodeo rough stock, work on big-rig trucks, and helped you at the store, from what I understand."

"Yeah, but…"

"But nothing. He can't do those things anymore and may not *ever* be able to again. And what about making love to you? What if he can't? How would that make you feel?"

"Pretty helpless."

"Exactly."

"I don't care about those things, though. I love him no matter whether he can walk or not."

"I'm sure that's true, but you have to convince him."

She shook her head. "I don't know if I can, Chase. What if he won't let me?"

"Listen to Abby. She knows him pretty well, and she can tell you just how stubborn I was." A soft chuckle left his mouth. "That will give you a good clue into Cole's personality."

Once they returned to the house, Chase left to work with one of the horses, leaving Abby and her inside.

"Let me tell you how Chase and I met. I've never seen a more stubborn man and trust me, Cole isn't any different as far as that goes." Abby told her the story of how she and Chase and fought their attraction for each other, and she had to laugh. "The first I met Cole, I didn't have hardly any clothes on."

"You're kidding me."

"No." Abby blushed. "Chase and I were here in the living room. One of the horses had kicked him and broken his leg. I kept trying to help him, but he could be so damned stubborn. He drove me nuts!"

Carrie chuckled.

"Don't ask me why, but I volunteered to play cards with Chase. Somehow," Abby cleared her throat, "somehow we managed to end up playing strip poker."

"Strip poker?"

"Yeah. Anyway, we finally gave in to the desire that raged between us every time we were in the same room." Abby's blush deepened. "We hadn't gotten dressed yet when Cole pulled into the driveway and came busting through the door. I didn't have a shirt on. Embarrassed is too mild a word, but what really shocked the hell out of me was the fact that he looks so much like my former husband, it's eerie sometimes." She revealed to Carrie how she lost her first husband in the Twin Tower bombings, and they cried together as Carrie told her about her parents and Jess.

"You've been through the ringer in the last couple of years."

Carrie gave Abby a watery smile. "Yeah, you could say that, but when Cole was there for me after Jess died…"

"You fell in love with him."

"Yeah. Even though I knew he might not be around, I didn't have a lot of choice. My heart wasn't listening very well."

"I know what you mean. That stubborn organ tends to do whatever it wants to. The Wilder men tend to bring out the best in the right woman."

Carrie shrugged. "I didn't want to fall in love with him, Abby. It just complicated things, and I'm not sure I have it in me to fight him if he doesn't want to be with me."

"That's just it. He does."

"How do you know?"

"I've seen it in the way he looks at you—like you're something precious and he's afraid he'll do something to screw up and you'll walk away. Now, he's going to push you away because he thinks that's what is best for you."

"How am I going to convince him being with him *is* what's best for me?"

A mischievous smile lifted Abby's lips at the corners. "I'll have a little talk with him. Now, let's go shopping."

Several hours later, the two women sat in a small coffee shop in the mall with several bags sitting in a chair next to them.

"Chase is going to kill you for buying more clothes."

"Nah." Abby waved her hand in a dismissing gesture. "He loves me, and he's not going to tell me no when it comes to things for his son."

Carrie cocked an eyebrow when a small smile lifted the corners of her lips. "His son? Have you had an ultrasound to tell you it's a boy?"

Abby stuck a spoonful of ice cream in her mouth as her own smile flashed across her face. "Don't need one."

"You can tell it's a boy?"

"Yeah."

"Mother's intuition?"

"No." Carrie stared and Abby laughed. "Just a feeling."

"Your kids will never be able to get away with anything."

"I didn't during my childhood, why should they?" Abby chuckled again before she stuck more ice cream in her mouth and sighed heavily. "I just love ice cream." She put the spoon down and said, "Now, let's talk about Cole and you."

"What if I can't convince him he's being a jackass about this whole thing and the best thing for me is to be with him? What will I do if he turns his back on me?"

"Even if he does, it will only be for a short time. He loves you, and eventually he'll come to his senses and realize he can't live without you."

"I wish I could believe that."

"Believe it, girl. As long as I've known Cole, I have never seen him act like he does around you."

Carrie shrugged. "I don't know how you can be so sure."

Abby smiled while she cocked her head slightly and said, "Just a feeling."

* * * *

That afternoon, Carrie walked into his room, and he frowned. "I thought I told you not to come back this afternoon."

"What's your point?" She cocked an eyebrow as her gaze raked him from head to toe, before she settled into the chair at his side.

"You obviously don't listen very well."

"I haven't before, so what makes you think I would start now?"

A dry chuckle left his lips. "That's the Carrie I know and love."

The surprised gasp that left her mouth made him realize what he said, and he shifted his gaze away from her lest she read the truth in his eyes.

She picked up his hand in hers, cradling his palm, letting the warmth of his touch penetrate the ice she felt radiating from him. "Do you?"

"Do I what?"

"Look at me, Cole."

Biting his lip, he finally turned back to face her.

"Look me in the eyes and tell me you don't love me. If you can do that, I'll go back home and you'll never see me again."

He stiffened and pulled his hand from hers. "Go home, Carrie. I don't need you here."

The pain in her eyes sliced his heart to shreds. He thought for sure she was going to cry, and if she did, he'd be a goner, but she pulled her shoulders back and retreated.

"Fine. I'm glad we got this straightened out." He could see the tears pooling in the corners of her eyes until anger took their place. "I really thought you might be different, you know? Not the typical rodeo guy, but I guess I was wrong. You just use people and throw them to the side when you're done. Well, I'm through being your port in the storm. If you would rather wallow in self-pity than pull yourself up by your bootstraps and let someone who loves you help you, then that's fine. I'm done." She turned and headed for the door.

"Carrie…"

Reaching the door, she turned back for a moment before she said, "Don't, Cole. I don't need your rejection. I've had enough of it to last me a lifetime."

Then she was gone.

* * * *

"You, Cole Wilder, are an ass!" Abby stomped into his room, rage written across her pretty features.

"Thanks, Abby. I appreciate the sentiment."

"Why did you do that?"

"Do what?"

"Let her walk away?"

"She's gone?"

"Yes. I took her to the airport myself. I did everything I could to get her to stay."

He wouldn't look her in the face anymore as he turned to peer out the window at the softly falling snow. "I don't want her here, Abby. I don't need her here." His hands were balled into fists, lying next to his hips on the bed.

"And you are one of the biggest liars I've ever had the pleasure of meeting. Somehow you convinced her you don't love her, but I know that's not true."

"I don't."

"You can try to lie to yourself, Cole, but I've seen the way you look at her. I hope you are happy living the rest of your life alone when you could have been with the one woman who turns your life upside down and inside out."

That's one way to put it—upside down and inside out.

"She loves you, too, stubborn jackass!"

"No, she doesn't. She just thinks she does."

"How can you lie there and know what's in her heart? If she said she loved you, then she does. Why won't you believe her?"

"Because I don't want to tie her to a man that may never walk again, may never be able to make love to her again. She's better off finding someone who can be everything for her and not be another burden in her life. She doesn't need that. She needs a man who can love her like I can't, like Justin."

"Justin. You're kidding right?"

"No."

"She's not even attracted to Justin, she loves you." Abby's voice got soft when she pulled up the chair next to him and took his hand in hers. "You think you would be a burden?"

He couldn't look at her as the tears threatened to choke him. "Yeah. She already has to raise her nephew because of Jessica's death, plus take care of the store and keep up the property. She doesn't need me to complicate things for her."

"Cole, don't you understand. She would rather have you with her, no matter what capacity it is. She loves you. She doesn't want to be alone."

"She wouldn't be alone for long, Abby, and you know that. Hell, there were several guys in Silver Ridge who were chasing her even when I was there, and I'm sure most of them would give their left nut to be with her."

"But you aren't one of them."

He finally turned back and chuckled dryly. "I would give up both."

"So you think by letting her find someone else you are doing what's best for her. Is that right?"

"Yes," he whispered, his gaze returning to the window.

"Well, for what it's worth, you are making the biggest mistake of your life, and I hope you realize that some day."

Abby stood and walked out the door without another word.

"You have no idea, Abby—you have no idea," he whispered to the empty room as a small tear slid down his cheek.

* * * *

"Hey, babe."

Carrie rolled her eyes when she heard the familiar drawl behind her.

He never gives up, does he?

"What can I get for you, Ken?"

"I think we've had this conversation before, several times in fact."

"Yeah, I'm pretty sure we have, and the answer is still the same. I'm not interested."

She looked around the store while the sunshine filtered through the blinds. Summer had arrived and so had the customers along with the rodeo.

I can't believe it's been an entire year since I first met Cole.

She shook her head. No use dwelling on what can't be. It had been six long months since she walked out of his life and he let her.

She'd hired more help so she could spend her days taking care of Robert since Jimmy did nothing for his son, but she still had to do the books. Today, one of her workers called in sick, so she brought the baby with her and stood manning the counter. She smiled when she looked at the little boy in the playpen who just learned to roll over.

"So what ever happened to your boyfriend? You know the one who was hanging around for a while?"

She frowned. Cole often found his way into her thoughts, but she pushed him aside. He had made his choice, and she had made hers. Her life was in Silver Ridge, taking care of Robert and running the store. Maybe someday she would find someone to love like she loved him, but she doubted it. Her heart continued to be wrapped around his little finger, just like it had been from the moment he flashed those delicious dimples in her direction. The fact that she hadn't seen him or talked to him in a very long time didn't matter. He would forever be in her heart.

A frustrated sigh slipped from between her lips. "Does it matter?"

"Yeah. I'm curious if I have competition or not."

She chuckled and picked up the baby. "You don't have competition, Ken. You don't have anything other than wishful thinking. I'm not interested. I don't want to be with you, and I don't know how to make it any clearer."

"How about if you tell him you're in love with someone else?"

She gasped and spun around. Standing slightly behind Ken was the one man she thought she'd never seen again. "Cole…"

Chapter Seventeen

She took a step in his direction but stopped. "What are you doing here?"

"Why else would I be here? I came to see you."

Carrie took in everything about him. His hair was slightly longer but the same dark blond, and his eyes were the same bright blue. "Wait! You can walk?"

A dry chuckle left his mouth. "Yeah. It seems there wasn't permanent damage after all."

Her heart thumped loudly, slamming against her ribs while she stared.

God, he looks good, too good.

Tearing her gaze from his, she turned around and put the baby back in his playpen. She took her time, trying to calm her racing heart, until he moved closer and stood next to her.

"Carrie?"

Squeezing her eyes closed when a large lump formed in her throat and tears burned the back of her eyelids, she fought the urge to throw herself into his arms and beg him not to leave. "What do you want, Cole?"

"You."

"What if I said that's not going to happen?"

"I would think you were lying," he said as his fingers brushed against her arm and goose bumps flittered across her skin. "You can't deny what's between us any more than I can. Believe me, I've tried."

"There's nothing between us. You made that clear before."

"Maybe I changed my mind."

"Well, I haven't. I'm not letting you break my heart again." She walked away, headed for the door. It was time to close the store. When all the customers left, she locked it and turned the sign. She sighed heavily before she turned around and headed back toward him. A shiver rolled down her spine as her eyes took in the handsome man in front of her, leaning against the counter with his arms across his chest like he wasn't going anywhere.

Shaking her head, she moved around to the register, grabbed the money, and slipped it into the bag before heading toward the office. After putting everything into the safe, she stood up and turned around only to find Cole right behind her.

Her eyes went wide when he slipped his hand into her hair, tugging softly until she tipped her head back and his mouth swooped down, taking hers in a heart-stopping kiss. Fitting his lips against hers, he traced the crease with his tongue until she groaned and opened for him. Clinging to his shoulders, she gave into the desire racing through her veins, desire that had been banked inside her, smoldering, until he set it ablaze with nothing more than a kiss. His lips moved from her mouth, across her cheek to nibble at her ear before his tongue slid down her neck.

"God, I've missed you," he growled before he nipped at the soft skin, making her shiver. His fingers worked the small straps of her tank top from her shoulder, following one down her arm with his lips. His mouth closed over one nipple, and she gasped as need zipped through her body, settling between her legs in a heady pool. He wrapped his arms around her, grabbing her ass with both hands, lifting her up and settling her on the desk. "Let me love you, Carrie."

She gasped when the words splashed over her like an ice cold shower. *Not "I love you." It's "Let me love you, Carrie." Just sex, that's all it is to him.*

She pushed against his chest until he let her go. "Get out your hands off me and get the hell out of my store," she spat while rage zinged through her, replacing the desire there a few moments ago. She pulled the straps of her shirt back over her shoulders, trying desperately to calm her overheated body.

He stepped back like she had slapped him. "What did I say?"

"I'm not one of your weekend playthings, Cole. If I wanted nothing more than a temporary man, it sure in the hell wouldn't be you."

"Weekend plaything? What the hell are you talking about, woman?"

"If you think you can just walk back into my life whenever you feel like it, you are full of shit! Now get out! I need to lock up and get the baby home and fed. Goodbye."

She turned her back on him, busying herself with something on the desk until she heard him stomp out of the office and the front door slam when he left.

Closing her eyes when pain tore through her chest, she gave in to the tears that burned behind her eyes with a tortured sob.

An hour later, she sat on the couch at the house feeding the baby his bottle when a knock sounded at the door. Mumbling under breath at the interruption, she struggled to stand up with the baby in her arms. Finally managing to get to her feet as the knock sounded again, she put the bottle on the table and lifted him to her shoulder. Patting his back, she headed for the door.

"Who is it?"

"It's Cole."

She tipped her head back and sighed. *Why in the hell can't he just leave me alone?* "Go away, Cole. I don't want to see you."

"I'm not leaving until we talk, Carrie, so you might as well let me in."

"Stubborn ass man," she grumbled before she slid the lock on the door, allowing him to enter. Her heart almost stopped in her chest when he pushed open the door. She had almost forgotten how he looked in his Wranglers and form-fitting T-shirt that molded to his muscular pecs. Her hands itched to touch him and she murmured, "Damn! Why does he have to be so gorgeous?"

His gaze swung to the baby in her arms. "Can I hold him? I haven't seen him in so long." She shrugged and handed him Robert, amazed at how gentle he was. "He's gotten so big."

She cocked an eyebrow in his direction before she headed back into the living room. "You haven't seen him since he was a week old. I would think he's huge compared to what he weighed back then."

"I didn't even get to see him when you were in Laramie." He smiled at the little boy as Robert grabbed his T-shirt in his small fist. "He looks like Jess."

"I know," she whispered, pain evident in her voice.

"I'm sure you miss her."

She frowned. "Of course I do—every day." She walked back to his side, taking the baby from him. "I'll be right back. It's bed time for him."

Taking her time getting Robert ready for bed, she almost hoped Cole would give up and leave before she came back downstairs. That wasn't the case. Reaching the bottom stair, she took in the sight of the man standing in her living room before he realized she was there. He could still make her heart race with nothing more than a look or a smile. Having him near again was sending her body into shock with the need that raced along her nerves.

He turned when he heard her, his eyes raking her from head to toe as a slow smile swept across his mouth. She sucked in a ragged breath when the need to lick those tempting indentations rocked through her.

She cleared her throat and moved toward the couch, taking one end while he took the other. "So talk."

"Damn, you're stubborn."

"If you thought you were just going to walk back into my life, forget it. I don't have time for your games, Cole, whatever they may be."

"I don't play games, Carrie, not with you."

She stood up and started to pace while rage ripped through her.

"That is such bull shit! I don't believe you! First you say you love me, and then you push me away. In fact, you tried shoving me at your brother. All because in some warped sense of stubborn pride, you wanted to do what was best for me. *I* know what's best for me, but you didn't even give me a chance to tell you I wanted nothing more than to be with you."

"I didn't want you to be saddled with…"

Hands on her hips, she faced him and spat, "With what, Cole? A man who couldn't walk?"

"Yes."

"Yet you didn't even bother to ask me what I wanted. I didn't matter to you that I only wanted you. People who care about each other work things out—together, but no, you wanted to pull some macho *I'm the man* thing."

"It did matter. How could I ask you spend the rest of your life with someone who couldn't take care of you? Or someone who might never be able to make love to you again?"

"I don't need you to take care of me. I can take care of myself, thank you very much. I have for several years now."

He stood up and moved toward her as a nervous tingle zipped down her arms. Grabbing her upper arms in his hands, he pulled her to his chest. "I didn't want you to have to do it alone. I've seen how you had to give up your dreams to man the store and take care of Jess. Now you have to take care of Robert, and I didn't want to give you one more burden to bear, Carrie. I wanted to be the person who took care of you for a change. I wanted to shoulder some of those things for you, not add to them."

Tears clouded her vision while she stared into his eyes. "Don't you see," she sobbed. "I love you. I felt like I was dying when I saw you in that hospital bed and you couldn't talk to me. I thought I was going to lose you like I lost my parents and Jess. I prayed so hard that

God wouldn't take you from me too. At that point, the store didn't matter—only you mattered, but you turned your back on me."

"I'm sorry," he whispered, wrapping his hands around her until they stood chest to breast and thigh to thigh. His hands roamed down her back in a slow caress.

"I was so happy when you said you loved me, but then you pushed me away. I didn't know what to think."

"It doesn't matter now." He set her away from him and looked into her eyes as his fingers caressed her face. "I love you. I want to be there for you for the rest of our lives, to love you and help you."

She choked back a sob. "What about the rodeo stuff? I don't want someone who is only around during the week and gone off to God knows where on the weekends."

"I can't ride anymore—not rodeo, anyway. I can still work on trucks to help with bills, but my pro-rodeo days are over." The corners of his mouth lifted in a smile. "I can still trail ride."

"Why?"

"The doctor's said my back isn't perfect. If I were to chance it and get hurt again, I wouldn't be able to walk for the rest of my life. I don't want to risk losing you for anything in the world. You mean too much to me."

"Exactly what are you saying, Cole?"

He brushed the tears from her cheeks with his thumb. "I'm saying I love you, Carrie Marsh. Abby told me once that it would be sooner rather than later when I would run into the one woman who would put me in my place. I laughed at her. I figured there was no way I'd find someone I wanted to spend the rest of my life with because I wasn't in one place long enough. Leave it to you to wrap me around your little finger in two days. I can't live without you. I don't want to."

The next thing she knew, his lips were softly caressing hers. Nipping at the corners of her mouth, he trailed them along her cheek to her ear.

"Say you still love me, Carrie. I need you not just in my bed, but in my life, too."

"I love you. I never stopped. I couldn't even if I wanted to."

He lifted his head and looked into her eyes, giving her the biggest smile she'd ever seen. "Does that mean you'll marry me?"

She laughed and tears rolled down her cheeks. "Is that supposed to be a proposal?"

"It's the best I can do on short notice. I didn't know whether you would even see me, much less let me propose. There is one thing I can do, though," he said as he slid down her body, kissing her breasts and her stomach before reaching his knee. He slipped the ring off his pinky finger. "Carrie, will you marry me?"

"Yes," she whispered when he slid the ring on her left hand, and they both laughed.

"We'll go buy a pretty diamond tomorrow, but I wanted you to know tonight that I want you for my wife."

He stood up and swept her up in his arms, before he headed for the stairs, taking them two at a time until he reached her bedroom door. With a wicked grin, he said, "I've been thinking of this for months."

Epilogue

Robert giggled when Cole chased him around the furniture. Bonnie sat on the couch laughing at her son playing with the little boy while she cradled her other grandson in her arms. Samantha sat on her grandfather's lap and she read him a story.

"Can I get you anything, Bonnie?"

"Mother, please, Carrie."

She smiled her heart light with having her family around her. "All right, can I get you anything, Mother?"

"No sweetheart, I'm fine."

"I need something, though, wife of mine." Cole laughed before he swept her up in his arms.

Her arms wrapped around his shoulders. "And what would that be?"

"A kiss."

"I think I can manage one of those."

His mouth dove for hers as she sighed and pressed against him. He let his tongue caress the crease of her lips, asking for her mouth, which she gave up eagerly.

"All right, you two—enough of that," Chase said slapping Cole on the back.

"Carrie? I think this pie is done," Abby called from the kitchen. Carrie sighed as she flashed her husband a devious smile and backed toward the kitchen. He started to follow until Chase stopped him. She giggled at the disappointed look on his face.

"We've been assigned to set the table."

"You are absolutely no fun at all, Chase. I'm still a newlywed, for crying out loud."

Chase laughed and handed him the plates from the china hutch.

Jamie, Abby, and Carrie began to bring out the mountain of food that they had been preparing for days for the family's Thanksgiving. She and Cole managed to convince all of them to come to Silver Ridge for the holiday. When everything was in place, Cole took the head of the table with Carrie to his right and the rest of his family around him.

He took Carrie's hand in his, giving her a playful wink before he turned his attention back to the rest of his family.

"I know I have a lot of be thankful for this year, and I want to share some of those with you all. First, I thank God every day for bringing Carrie into my life. I don't know how I survived before I met her."

"With a hell of a lot of luck," Justin piped in.

They all laughed.

"Very true, Justin. Just wait until you find a woman who turns your life upside down." Cole winked at Abby as a knowing smile spread across her lips. Carrie told Cole about her conversation with Abby the night before. Carrie knew Abby already had one of her feelings about the woman Justin would find and fall helplessly in love with. He just didn't know it yet. Carrie almost rubbed her hands together gleefully as she thought about Justin being put in his place. He had to be one of the most arrogant, domineering, and stubborn men she ever met.

Cole cleared his throat. "Second, I need to thank all of you for being there for me when I wasn't sure I would ever walk again and had shut out the one person I shouldn't have."

"I forgive you." A smirk settled on her lips, and she cocked a knowing eyebrow in his direction. "You'll pay for that later."

Another round of laughter echoed in the dining room, and Carrie sighed happily. It had been such a long time since there had been this much happiness around her, and she loved every minute of having her adopted family close.

"Thirdly, I need to thank my wife. She's stood by me and loved me, stubborn man that I am…through these past months and my need to come to terms with the changes in my life." He kissed the hand he held, his blue eyes sparkling with mischief. "And we need to let you all know in about eight months, there will be another Wilder in the family."

"You're pregnant?"

"Well, I'm not, but Carrie is." He joked at his mother's question when his gaze caressed Carrie's face until she was tugged to her feet. His family wrapped her in warm hugs of congratulations before his brothers slapped him on the back.

"Now—shall we eat?"

Laughter rang throughout the room when Cole cut the turkey and everyone piled their plates high with food.

THE END

www.romancestorytime.com

ABOUT THE AUTHOR

Sandy Sullivan is a romance author, who, when not writing, spends her time with her husband Shaun on their farm in middle Tennessee. She loves to ride her horses, play with their dogs and relax on the porch, enjoying the rolling hills of her home south of Nashville. County music is a passion of hers and she loves to listen to it while she writes.

She is an avid reader of romance novels and enjoys reading Nora Roberts, Jude Deveraux and Susan Wiggs. Finding new authors and delving into something different helps feed the need for literature. A registered nurse by education, she loves to help people and spread the enjoyment of romance to those around her with her novels. She loves cowboys so you'll find many of her novels have sexy men in tight jeans and cowboy boots.

Also by Sandy Sullivan

Cowboy Love
Wilder Series 1: *Wild Wyoming Nights*
Wilder Series 3: *Wild Nevada Ride*
Wilder Series 4: *Wild Rekindled Love*
BookStrand Mainstream: *Love's Sweet Surrender*

Available at
BOOKSTRAND.COM

Siren Publishing, Inc.
www.SirenPublishing.com

Breinigsville, PA USA
22 June 2010
240418BV00005B/141/P